THE HANDYMAN HOMICIDE

LIBBY HOWARD

LIBBY HOWARD
WHODUNNITS WITH HEART

CHAPTER 1

"You might want to change the name." Mom pointed up at the wooden sign as we drove under it. "Reckless Camper Campground. It doesn't exactly instill confidence in the safety of the encampment. It implies there are inherent dangers in staying here."

"Reckless is the name of the town," I reminded her. She was right, though. Reckless Camper Campground conjured up images of sinking boats, marauding bears, and tent fires—the sorts of accidents that would get an insurance liability policy cancelled.

Maybe I *should* change the name. But not now. I had way too much to do now just getting our new purchase spruced up for the fast-approaching camping season. A name change would mean new signs, and a new website URL at the very least. Who knew what other stuff would require replacing. I didn't have a whole lot in the bank account after writing that big down-payment check this morning, which meant I'd have to carefully prioritize our spending.

I continued on down the drive, past the overgrown brown grass of the tent and RV lots to the rows of cabins that flanked a log home, the glistening blue lake in the background.

"What have I done?" I breathed as I parked the Explorer and climbed out.

It was a rhetorical question. I knew exactly what I'd done. I had sold my home and sunk every penny I had in this place. Sight unseen—at least unseen for the last thirty years. I'd uprooted my eighty-five-year-old mother, who'd been comfortably living with me since my father's death ten years ago, to spend the rest of her golden years at a *campground*. Admittedly, Mom seemed ridiculously enthusiastic about this new adventure, but I still worried how she'd fare in our new home.

Anxiety gnawed at my stomach. I took a deep breath, blew it out, and felt myself relax. I'd loved this campground as a child. I'd loved it the times I'd brought my son here on vacation. In my darkest moments, I'd dreamed of owning a place like this. I'd swim in the lake, hike on the trails, watch the sun set over the mountains. I'd provide the same amazing vacation experiences for others that I'd had both as a child and as an adult.

I'd never wear a suit again.

Not quite two years ago, I'd feared those dreams would be gone forever. But I had a second chance at life—a chance to do all the things I'd dreamed of but put off. Life was short and precious, and I didn't want to go to my maker with my dreams unfulfilled.

I'd vowed to take more risks, to live every day as if it were a gift—because it was. Maybe I should have started small, like learning Swedish or taking up fly-fishing, not liquidating my assets and purchasing the campground of my happy child-hood vacations. But this campground *meant* something to me. It meant peace, beauty, joy, and family—all the things I wanted to prioritize going forward.

If I didn't start living my dreams now, I might not have time to do so in the future.

I heard a low growly-bark from the SUV and turned. My dog, Elvis, decided I wasn't fast enough in opening the rear door for him and took matters into his own paws, clambering over the center console to the driver's seat, then hopping out to land beside me. After a full-body shake that sent his long ears flopping around his head and drool flying, the dog dropped his snout to the ground and began to explore.

Bloodhounds. To them the most important things in the world were at the end of their noses. I sniffed the fresh air and thought that Elvis might be right.

"Oh, Sassy!" My mother rounded the front of the Explorer and spun around with her arms wide, like an elderly Maria from *The Sound of Music*. "It's exactly like it was when you and Quint were little and your dad and I brought you here. Beautiful. So very beautiful."

My idealistic visions of this place moved to the side so the pragmatic Corporate America me could take a good hard look around.

Beautiful wasn't exactly the adjective Corporate Me would use to describe Reckless Camper Campground right at this moment. It *could* be beautiful. With some hard work and creativity, this could be the place of my dreams. But now...

Mom and I were glass-always-full people. Just being here, inhaling the crisp scent of cold lake water, the early spring flowers, and pine needles brought back a flood of memories. My brother, Quint, and I had loved our family camping trips. And the times when I'd brought my son Colton here had been magic. I'd always loved this place, and looking around I could still see the bones of the place of my dreams. It was right there, under a layer of dust and neglect, waiting for me to bring it back to glorious life.

It would take a lot of work, but I was ready for that—eager even.

The campground had been closed since the owner's death this fall, so I should have expected the weed-choked grounds and the dirty walkways. I *hadn't* expected the gutter hanging off the corner of the owner's house, or the fallen tree that was resting on the roof on what I assumed was cabin number six.

Some premonition shivered up my back. Not about the fallen tree or the gutter. I frowned, looking over at the three cabins to the right of the owner's house. Something felt...wrong.

I shook it off, chalking the feeling up to a mixture of excitement over my purchase, nerves over the move, and a lack of breakfast.

"It needs some work," Mom said, echoing my thoughts. "But it's beautiful."

It was, and I was ready to get started cleaning, organizing, and planning for this year's camping season. I knew going into this that the campground of my dreams would need a lot of TLC and sweat equity. That was the only reason I'd even been able to afford this place.

The current deferred maintenance issues shouldn't be a problem. After all, it was only April 1st. I could do this and be ready for the early spring campers that should be arriving in the next week.

Correction—*Mom* and I could do this. As she'd reminded me over the last week, we were partners, and she was just as emotionally invested in this new venture as I was.

Leonard Trout had owned and managed this campground for sixty-three years. He'd kept the business going after his kids had grown and gone. He'd kept it going after the death of his wife, running the place single handedly with the help of a part-time handyman. If Len Trout could operate this campground well into his eighties, then Mom and I shouldn't have any problem.

"Yes. It's beautiful." It *would* be beautiful. When I was done with this place, it would shine. We'd be booked a year in advance. People would talk for decades about how much fun they'd had that summer they stayed at Reckless Camper Campground.

Just as I'd done.

My mother smiled serenely, taking it all in with a sweeping glance. "How about you start unloading the car while I go check out the cabins."

We hadn't packed much. The movers would be here tomorrow, and the place had been sold along with all the business equipment and furnishings. We hadn't been sure what would fit in the owner's house, or what we'd want to toss, so we'd had movers throw everything from our old house onto the truck, figuring we'd sort it all out when they got here.

Mom headed toward the first cabin with a pace that belied her age. Elvis's sniffing was leading him on a path toward the owner's house. I grabbed my keys and pushed the button to open the back lift, then walked around to grab our bags. That's when I saw her.

A woman with a poofy blonde mullet that belonged back in 1983 was speed walking up the packed-dirt driveway. She wore a bright coral jacket paired with jade green pants and was carrying something that looked like one of those giant Edible Arrangement baskets.

"Yoohoo! Yooooo-hoooooo!" She took one hand off the basket to wave at me and increased her speed. I had no idea a person could walk that fast. She reminded me of those Standardbred horses who looked like they were trotting sixty miles an hour around a racetrack.

I put down the box I'd picked up and waited for her. I was tired from the long drive and emotionally exhausted after an incredibly busy morning. I needed to unpack the SUV, get the essentials organized, and begin figuring out where we were going to put our furnishings. But I was new here and I welcomed any overtures of friendship.

Especially when they were speed walking up the driveway carrying a basket of food.

"Halooooo!" The woman came to an abrupt stop in front of me and breathlessly extended the basket. In addition to the fruit arrangement, I realized the basket contained muffins, mini loaves, and chocolates.

Chocolates. Whoever this woman was, she was my new best friend.

"I'm Lottie Sinclair from next door," she panted at me. "I saw your car pull in and just *had* to be the first to welcome you to the neighborhood."

She said it as if welcoming newcomers to the neighborhood was a competitive event here in Reckless.

"I'm Sassafras Letouroux," I juggled the basket so I could shake her hand. "Everyone calls me Sassy. My mother, Ellie Mae Letouroux is…somewhere."

Mom was nowhere to be seen. She'd probably ducked into one of the cabins to check it out. Glancing around, I saw Elvis sniffing along the front porch of the owner's house. Bloodhounds could vanish with an instant of inattention, following their nose clear across the darned country if they were on a scent, so I needed to keep an eye on him.

"I'm so glad you bought the campground. Len was a wonderful man, God rest his soul." She made the sign of the cross on her chest. "It's not healthy for a place to be vacant for long. And this campground needs someone to love it—

someone who really cares, someone whose aura is aligned with the spirit of this place."

That was a bit on the woo-woo side for me, but I *did* really care about this campground. It had seemed like fate that in the exact moment when I'd been wanting to change my life and take a chance on something new, the very place I'd adored as a child had come up for sale—and at a price I could actually afford.

"I came here quite a few times when I was a kid and always loved it here," I told Lottie, envisioning how the campground had looked back then. "And I brought my son when he was little as well."

"Then you're practically a Reckless native," she proclaimed.

I laughed. "Ten visits over the course of fifty-eight years hardly makes me a native."

"Close enough." She waved her hand. "We were all so worried some developer was going to snatch it up and slap a bunch of condos here, or someone would buy it, raze everything, and put up a million-dollar mansion with locked gates and butlers." She eyed me. "You're not planning to do that, are you?"

"No. I intend to live in the owner's cabin with my mom and my dog, and manage the campground." She should be able to tell from my clothes and my old model SUV that I wasn't the million-dollar home type, but maybe the millionaires around Reckless didn't flaunt their wealth.

"Oh, good." Lottie continued to talk, naming off everyone on either side of the street for a mile or so, and telling me what they did for a living as well as if they were married and had children or pets. I stood there, half listening to her, half keeping an eye on Elvis who I didn't trust not to vanish into the mountains following the scent of a rabbit or a fox or a dog in heat. The rescue had him neutered before I'd adopted him, but Elvis clearly hadn't gotten the memo. Any female dog within a mile would have him courting her favor with his baritone hound-song.

I put the bags down and set the goodie basket in the rear of the SUV, because Lottie didn't seem to be letting up her monologue anytime soon, and my arms were getting tired. My mom was making her way back up the path from the cabins. Elvis had moved on from the porch of the house to the door of what might be a freestanding garage.

"...bridge every Tuesday, then there's Cocktail Chicks Thursdays, and Knit-O-Rama ever Saturday..."

"Bridge sounds lovely. It's been ages since I've played, though." Mom put her hand out to shake Lottie's. "I'm Ellie Mae Letouroux."

I'd never played bridge, but mom and dad had when I was back in high school. I vaguely remembered coming home from the roller rink or football games and finding a dozen people in our living room, all seated at those fold-up card tables. I'd never been sure if my parents had truly loved the card game, or had just used it as an excuse to get together with friends, drink martinis, and eat those little hot dogs rolled up in Crescent rolls that Mom used to bake for parties.

"Lottie Sinclair. I live right next door." Lottie shook mom's hand and pointed over her shoulder in the direction of the woods. The campground was twenty acres, so next door wasn't exactly spitting distance, but I could vaguely see a roofline just over the tops of the trees.

Lottie threw her hands upward. "Goodness sakes, here I am chatting your ear off and you haven't even unpacked yet."

I expected Lottie to say goodbye, but instead she reached in and grabbed a bag with each hand. The last few years I'd learned to accept help when offered, so I grabbed another two bags while Mom took the goodie basket and we walked to the owner's house. It took me a few seconds of fumbling with the janitor-sized ring of keys the real estate agent had given me before I found the correct one and got the door unlocked. The door creaked open, and I wrinkled my nose, thinking that the place could use a good airing out and a going-over with some Febreze.

The owner's house was a one-story log cabin with an open floor plan. There was a floral-print sofa in front of a stone fireplace. The previous owners clearly hadn't wanted it enough to keep and hadn't bothered to haul it off. I grimaced, my fingers itching to grab the tags that would mark this sofa as something that should be hauled away for donation. Heck, I wasn't even sure Goodwill would take it. It wasn't ratty or faded, just old, with that heavy dark-wood structure and dated upholstery. I was nostalgic, but my love of things past didn't extend to mid-century Early Americana furnishings.

On either side of the fireplace were floor-to-ceiling bookshelves packed two deep with books.

The kitchen had what looked like the same autumn gold appliances from my childhood in the early '70s. As much as I wanted those to go out the door with the sofa, I didn't really have the budget to replace perfectly good, albeit ugly, appliances. They'd need to stay, and I'd just have to put up with Harvest Gold.

To the left of the kitchen was a heavy, oak farmhouse-style dining table with two chairs that had been repaired with duct tape. I eyed the table, noting that it had survived all sorts of gouges and broken chunks of wood. It looked sturdy enough to tap dance on. Even if I decided not to keep it in the main house, I could repurpose it in the campground office, or possibly in the activities center.

Off to the side of the table was a desk with a computer on it. Now *that* was supposed to be here. All the rest of these furnishings were not. I took a deep breath, annoyed that Len

Trout's sons had abandoned all this junk for us to deal with and that our real estate agent hadn't given us a heads-up.

I set the bags on the kitchen island, mentally adding "arrange for a junk hauler to pick this all up and haul it away" to my to-do list as I continued to inspect the place that Mom and I would now be calling home.

I knew there were two bedrooms in the back with one full bath. There was also a nice enclosed porch off the dining area. Everything else was in the one big room. The cabin was cozy, but it was just Mom and me who'd be living here. And Elvis. We hadn't exactly lived in fancy digs before this adventure, but the owner's house was a whole lot more rustic than either of us was used to. Nothing that couldn't be spruced up a bit with some bright accents, though. It wasn't like we'd be roughing it. The whole campground had electricity, well water, and a septic system. There was indoor plumbing, heat, and hot water in our new home. I hadn't bought this place expecting a glitzy house. It was a campground, after all, and I'd known it wouldn't be luxurious.

It was home. We could always remodel if we wanted, but that would have to be a year or two down the road. I got the feeling there would be a whole lot more important stuff for us to handle getting this place up and running and earning money before we worried about whether to buy new appliances or add a half-bath.

"Where should I put these bags?" Lottie wheeled them down the hallway without waiting for direction.

It wouldn't really matter which bedroom she put them in. Mom and I would figure out who got which one later. Right now my priority was getting the luncheon meat and drinks from the coolers into the house and into the refrigerator, inventorying essentials like toilet paper and cleaning supplies, then firing up that ancient computer over in the corner to see when our first reservation of the season was.

The cabins would require cleaning and to be stocked with amenities and linens. I should also figure out what needed to be done to prep the RV sites. The tent spots shouldn't be a problem, but I still wanted to check and make sure they were neat and tidy. Mow. Power wash the walkways. And there were four shower-and-restroom buildings that would need cleaning. The docks. The canoes and kayaks. Make sure there were no old wasp nests in the campsite grills. Have someone come in to cut up and haul away that downed tree and fix the roof in Cabin six. And reattach the gutter.

My chest tightened, and I felt light-headed at the overwhelming number of tasks ahead of me. Mom's responsibilities would be more on the organization and reservations side of our business venture. I was the one who was supposed to be coming up with creative events, doing the marketing and promotion, and coordinating campground activities with the town.

In all my daydreams, I'd never once thought about who would be cleaning, landscaping, and unclogging toilets. Was that the job of the part-time maintenance man? Daryl Butts, I think his name was. If so, then why hadn't any of this been done prior to our arrival? Had Len's sons fired the maintenance guy or reduced his hours to save money? Did Daryl just start slacking off once Len had died?

Or maybe none of this was in his job description, so Daryl had just ignored the cleaning, the tree on top of cabin six, and the sagging gutter on the owner's house. I moved "having a meeting with the maintenance man" to the top of my list, vowing to call him first thing in the morning and figure out what exactly he was supposed to do around here, and what I'd need to hire someone else to handle. Or to do myself.

Lottie came back from the bedrooms, dusting her hands

off and looking around. "Do you have more to unload?" she asked cheerfully.

"I'm very grateful for your help," I told her. "There are some coolers, a few other bags, and a couple more suitcases, if you don't mind giving us a hand."

"It's not a problem at all. I'm happy to help." She smiled, and we followed her outside, Lottie quickly outpacing us with her speedy walk.

Our neighbor grabbed one of the coolers and another bag. I picked up a box with paper goods and a bag of dog food, and suddenly realized I hadn't been keeping an eye on my bloodhound.

"Elvis!" I shouted, before turning to Mom and Lottie. "Have either of you seen Elvis?"

"He went around back when we were bringing in that last load," Lottie said.

"Elvis!" I shouted again, a wave of relief washing over me as the hound bounded around the house toward us. Hounds liked to follow their nose, and who knows what Elvis's nose would lead to around here. I really needed to keep a better eye on him. It wouldn't be a great first day if I had to spend it searching the mountains for my bloodhound, worried that he might have gotten himself into trouble.

Elvis followed us back and forth as we carried our things into the house. Lottie continued to chat about the neighbors and various events in the town. I made a mental note to write them down later, thinking the events would be good things to add to our website to entice campers to come. The previous owner's sons had given Mom and me the database of previous customers, the current year's upcoming reservations, all the finances for the business, and both the website and online booking system logins. Thankfully there were people who seemed to stay every summer because the new reservations had shown a steady decline over the last five years. I hoped I could reverse that trend.

"Would you stay and have a cup of coffee?" Mom asked Lottie as we made our final trip. "We only have instant—unless the previous owners left a coffee maker as well as that hideous couch."

"Not a chance," I said as I went through the empty cupboards.

"At least we brought a kettle to heat up water," Mom commented.

I nodded. "Looks like it's instant coffee in Styrofoam cups, but we've got real cream and little packets of sugar."

"And the fruit and muffins you brought," Mom said to Lottie.

"Please stay." I smiled at our new neighbor, grateful for her help and the gift basket.

She beamed back at me and smoothed a hand over her capris. "Oh, I'd love to!"

Lottie immediately bustled about, helping mom with the coffee and the muffins. Elvis explored the cabin, his nose to the floor as he inhaled all the scents this new place exuded. I sat down at the computer and fired it up, checking e-mails and looking at the booking system.

"We've got guests arriving next week for some of the cabins," I announced.

My chest tightened with a flash of panic. Were the cabins guest-ready? I was going to go out on a limb and say no. While I wanted to spend my first week here getting settled in, meeting the neighbors, exploring the town, and putting together a marketing plan, I was probably going to be cleaning, washing linens, and prepping the cabins for the early-spring guests.

"Didn't Len Trout have a handyman on the payroll?"

Mom asked. "Surely that man didn't climb up on roofs and repair plumbing at his age."

"Yes, he did," I replied. "But I don't know if roof and plumbing repair was something the handyman did or not."

"Daryl Butts," Lottie confirmed what I'd been told at signing. "Len's had him working here part-time for the last ten years. He felt sorry for Daryl after he got let go at the cannery in Bixby and offered him a job. Daryl's responsible for repairs on the cabins and docks, and groundskeeping. After Len died, the boys were paying him to look after the place."

I thought of the tree on cabin six's porch roof and wondered what Daryl's idea of "looking after the place" included.

"Of course, Daryl has to be in a working kind of mood, if you know what I mean," Lottie added, making a tippling motion with her hand.

"Is there another handyman in town?" I wasn't going to outright fire someone just because the place needed work and the neighbor I'd only met an hour ago implied the current handyman was a drinker. For all I knew, Len's estate hadn't paid the guy in months, or the sons had told him not to bother doing anything but a quick drive-through once a week. And Lottie's idea of a drinker could be a beer on Sunday after mowing the lawn. Still, it would be good to have a backup, just in case my fears about Daryl were proven true.

Lottie shrugged. "Not really. You could post on Reckless Neighbors and see if anyone's got a recommendation."

"Reckless Neighbors?" I typed the name into the search bar and saw it was some sort of messaging service for the town and outlying areas.

"That's the easiest way to know what's going on around

here." Lottie laughed. "That and sitting around The Coffee Dog listening to the locals chat."

Sadly, I wasn't going to have the time to hang around a coffee shop all day.

I signed up to the app, and by the time Mom and Lottie had set out muffins and cups of instant coffee at the battered dining room table, I'd already learned that the farmer's market was Thursdays from three to seven and ran all year long, rain or shine, and that pickleball teams were now forming with enrollment forms at the community center.

"Celeste Crenshaw lost her pig," I commented as I joined them at the table and grabbed one of the muffins.

Lottie waved a hand. "Squeakers is down at the Bait and Beer. You'd think Celeste would know that by now. She posts every time that pig goes missing just to have something to say. There's nothing else going on in her life."

"Maybe that's why Squeakers likes to hang out at the Bait and Beer," Mom chimed in.

"Celeste should probably *join* Squeakers at the Bait and Beer. Maybe then she'd have more things to post about on Reckless Neighborhood," I pointed out.

"That's true." Lottie sipped her coffee and looked off into the distance, her gaze pensive. "There's a lot that goes on at Bait and Beer."

I made a mental note to go check out Bait and Beer. Then I took a bite of the muffin and could have sworn I heard angels sing. "This is amazing. Lottie, did you make these? They're incredible."

Her face turned red and she waved my praise away. "Thank you. It's the blueberries. Those hippy ladies who run the llama sanctuary off route 31 sell them at the farmer's market the end of June. One week only. There's practically a riot going on with people line busting and camping out so they can get them. I scored three pints last year and froze some."

Hippy ladies. Llama sanctuary. The farmer's market. Bait and Beer. A wandering pig. Pickleball teams. Knit-O-Rama, and bridge, and Cocktail Chick Thursdays. I thought about all the interesting people, places, and events in Reckless. All this just confirmed that I was going to love living here.

I sipped my instant coffee, ate my muffin, and thought happy llama sanctuary thoughts while Mom and I got to know our neighbor.

"My son's in college," Lottie told Mom. "My daughter Amanda lives in Atlanta. She's a radiology technician. Aaron is majoring in history. I'm not sure what he's going to do with that, but he's a smart boy. He'll figure it out.

"He could teach," I pointed out. "Or do something completely different from history. My degree was in psychology and I ended up with a career in marketing."

She brightened at that. "True. Do you have children?"

"A son. Colter." I smiled just thinking of him. "He's thirty-two, married, and lives in Dallas with his partner. He works in software development. No grandkids yet, but Colter and Greg have been talking about adoption lately."

"No grandkids for me yet, either." Lottie sighed. "It's hard having an empty nest, isn't it? I'm lucky if I see Amanda every other Christmas. Aaron always gets jobs during the summer and stays on campus. The last time he was home was New Year's Day."

It *was* hard. I missed Colter, but he was off living his life and it made me proud that I'd raised an independent son who'd found love and had a wonderful job. He seemed so happy in the pictures he and Greg texted that I wouldn't change a thing, even if I did wish he'd found a job that wasn't over halfway across the country.

"Goodness! Look at the time! I need to get a-moving."

Lottie jumped to her feet. "I'm sure you both want to unpack and get settled in. Are you going to the tourism board meeting tomorrow afternoon? They're going over the themes for the summer festivals, and deciding which bands to book for the Apple Harvest Jubilee."

Summer festivals? I really needed to be there so I could coordinate the campground activities around what the town was offering, and maybe even piggyback on the themes. I glanced over at Mom and she waved a hand at me.

"Go. I'll finish any unpacking, wait for the movers, and make a list for the store," she informed me.

I glanced at the computer.

She huffed out a breath. "Don't you worry about that. I'm supposed to be handling the reservations—not you. Go."

"But the moving truck—"

"For Pete's sake, Sassy. I can tell movers where to put things and probably convince them to haul this ugly couch away. You go to this meeting tomorrow. It's important."

"I'll drive," Lottie offered. "That way I can introduce you to people and show you around town a bit. Pick you up at one?"

I smiled at her, grateful that fate had given me a friend literally minutes after I'd pulled down the driveway to my new home—my new life.

"Thank you. I really appreciate all of your help. And the gift basket." I walked her to the door as Mom gathered up the coffee cups and paper towels.

Lottie speed walked down the driveway, her arms swinging in time with her steps. I watched her go, then realized two things as I turned around.

The back door was ajar. And Elvis was nowhere to be seen.

CHAPTER 2

"*E*lvis!" I shouted, hoping he'd come running out of one of the bedrooms.

"Oh no!" Mom dropped the paper towels in the garbage bag and ran to the back door. "I must not have locked it. Elvis! Elvis, you come back here right now!"

I should have named my bloodhound Houdini. Within days of my adopting him he'd figured out how to paw at the handle to open the door. From there, he'd taken to unlatching screen doors, nosing open sliding glass doors, and even turning knobs with his mouth. The only way to keep him from roaming was to have a deadbolt thrown at all times.

I grabbed the leash, dug the remote control for the electronic collar out of my purse, and hit the vibrate button as I ran for the back door. "He probably went down to sniff around the docks," I told Mom—although I said it more to convince myself than her. He'd be fine. He couldn't have been gone that long. There were a gazillion interesting things to sniff around the campground. He probably hadn't strayed far.

"Hope he didn't get into that dead body in cabin three," Mom commented.

Dead body? A *dead body* in cabin three?

I jogged toward the lake, calling for my dog, and hitting the vibrate button on the remote. Yes, Mom's comment had thrown me off stride for about a second, but my dog took priority even over a dead body. In my weird brain logic, I'd figured that Elvis could be getting into trouble right now, while a dead body wasn't exactly going to get any deader.

And maybe I'd heard Mom wrong. Maybe she'd said there was a dropped bootie in cabin three, or a red birdy in cabin three, or something. Surely there couldn't be a body here, at a campground that hadn't been open for the last six months.

Elvis wasn't at the little building that housed the office and the camp store, so I kept going toward the lake. There was a boat dock flanked by two stands filled with kayaks and canoes, then two skinny fishing piers about fifty yards out on either side of the dock. I looked around the kayaks and canoes, then ran toward one of the shower/restroom buildings, worry eating away at my stomach.

Twenty acres was a lot, but Elvis was a bloodhound and they could cover a lot of ground once they got on the trail of something interesting. I should have made sure the doors were all locked. I should have been watching and not distracted by Celeste Crenshaw's missing pig and the pickleball team sign-ups. I needed to get some sort of fenced area in place sooner rather than later. And in the meantime, I needed to always keep Elvis either locked in the house or tethered to me on a leash.

"Elvis!" I rounded the shower house and was almost knocked flat by a wet, smelly, one-hundred-pound hound.

"Ugh, what have you gotten in to?" I clipped the leash onto his collar and wrinkled my nose at the odor coming off his fur. Wet, just-bathed hound was stinky, but wet, swamin-the lake hound was horribly stinky. Elvis might need to spend the night sleeping in the garage.

We walked back to where Mom was standing on the back porch, shouting for Elvis.

"Got him!" I called out.

I let go of the leash, and the hound ran to her. Mom bent down and ruffled Elvis's ears, telling him he was a naughty boy for worrying us. Elvis took that moment to shake his head, sending water as well as drool flying. We were used to it.

Live with a bloodhound, live with the drool.

"Mom, did you say there was a red bird in cabin three?" I tentatively asked, thinking now that my dog had been found safe and sound, I should get back to her earlier comment.

"No, dear. I said there's a dead body." Her voice was far too cheerful for that pronouncement.

"A dead body," I repeated, still not sure I'd heard her correctly.

"Yes, a dead body," she confirmed. "I'm no forensic technician, but I *have* watched a lot of CSI shows, and I'd say he hasn't been there very long. No more than a day, if Horatio Caine knows his stuff—and I do believe he does."

I blinked, wondering for a second who Horatio Caine was, then I remembered Mom's CSI reference.

"When were you planning on telling me about this dead body?" I asked, wondering why she'd returned from checking out the cabins, helped carry several loads of stuff into the house, made coffee and chatted with Lottie and me, but never thought to mention a corpse in one of the cabins?

"Well, I wasn't about to bring that up until after our guest left." She motioned to the driveway. "It didn't seem like a polite topic of conversation to have with someone you've just met, and it wasn't like he was going to get any deader. A dead body is no reason to be inhospitable, dear."

I let out a breath, feeling a little exasperated at my mother. Which probably wasn't fair given that I'd just had the same thoughts about the dead not getting any deader.

"Shall we go see?" Mom asked. "We could look for clues. Maybe I could find out what killed him if I got a better look at the body."

I held out my hands. "No. We're not going to go see. We're going to call the police, then we're going to wait."

Mom grumbled something under her breath. "Spoil sport. Fine. You take care of the police and the dead body. I'll take Elvis inside and start unpacking."

Dead body. It suddenly sunk in that there was a dead body in cabin three.

"I think I'll take Elvis with me, if you don't mind." I reached out and took his leash, then watched Mom climb the porch stairs. Elvis shook again, spraying me with more lake water. Keeping his leash tight in hand, I pulled my phone out of my jeans pocket, and dialed 911.

* * *

I PACED AROUND the front of the house, glancing over toward cabin three as I answered a list of questions about who I was, where I was, and what the nature of my emergency was.

"A dead body. In one of the cabins. At Reckless Camper Campground," the woman repeated.

I winced, recognizing that tone of disbelief. "Yes. I mean, I haven't seen the dead body myself. My mother was the one who saw it and she told me."

"You haven't checked yourself?" the operator asked.

"Uh, no. I haven't." I knew how that sounded. If someone said there was a dead body somewhere, a reasonable person should go to check it out, right? But I really, really didn't want to go.

"I'm not disturbing the sheriff or the deputy on a Sunday night for a prank call or a mistake," the operator informed me. "I need some firsthand knowledge here. Maybe you didn't hear your mother correctly and it was a red birdie or a dropped bootie and not a dead body. Why don't you go to cabin three and take a look. I'll stay on the line."

I really didn't want to go. It sounded horrible, but if I didn't go to cabin three, didn't see the actual body inside, I could pretend it wasn't real. I'd just bought this campground, just arrived here. And within the first hour, my mother had discovered a body. I wanted to pretend it wasn't true, to have the police show up and take care of everything without my even having to acknowledge what had happened.

But if there really was a body in cabin three…then it wasn't just a body, it was a person—a real person—who had died. He, or she, probably had concerned family worried about them, searching for them. They'd once been alive with thoughts, hopes, and dreams. I'd had my own brush with death not so long ago, and I felt a tug of emotion for this person. I couldn't just ignore them. That would be wrong.

So I put on my big-girl panties and headed toward the cabin, phone against my ear, and Elvis's leash in my hand. The hound was all about his nose, and I wasn't sure how his sensitive snooter would react to a dead body. But I couldn't waste time taking him back to the house to stay with Mom. With his sense of smell, he probably had already picked up the dead-body odor. And…I felt safer taking him with me.

Not because I needed canine protection from a deceased person, but because the thought of death scared me and I wanted something alive by my side when I confronted it.

I noticed as I climbed the steps that there were a few boards on the porch that were warped. I looked up and saw a hole in the roof. Grabbing the railing, I gently pulled and grimaced when it wiggled back and forth.

The campground had only been closed for six months, but these cabins seemed to have been neglected for longer than that. It didn't look like repairs had been done for quite a while, and it didn't look like anyone had been checking in on the place. Heck, I was surprised the owner's house hadn't been vandalized.

I'd need to post on that Reckless Neighbor site for a new handyman, because I wasn't skilled enough to do this sort of repair and Daryl Butts didn't seem to be up to the task if this was an example of his handiwork.

I added cabin three porch to my mental to-do list.

"Hello? Are you still there?" The irritated voice of the 911 operator rang out in my ear.

"Sorry. I had to walk across to the cabin. Sorry." I grimaced, staring at the door and steeling myself for what I might see inside.

Walking carefully across the porch, I grabbed the handle and turned it. It was unlocked, which worried me. Vandals could have come and robbed the place blind—vandals who had a propensity for fifty-year-old floral print couches and 1970s autumn gold appliances. Still, I didn't like the idea of vagrants possibly shacking up in the cabins over the winter, aware that the place was closed and up for sale by the non-resident sons of the deceased owner. If there was in fact a dead body, and not a red bird, in this cabin, that's probably who it was. Some homeless person who'd sadly died, alone, un-mourned, with no one even realizing he was gone.

That line of thinking had me tearing up, so I shoved the thoughts into the back of my mind, and walked into the cabin.

There were twelve of them at Reckless Camper Camp-ground—cabins that was, not dead bodies. The real estate agent had only Facetimed the inside of one, claiming that they were all identical. They were no-frills lodging, with one large room that held a bed, a dresser, two upholstered chairs with a table and lamp between them, and a small fireplace. On the roofed porch outside each cabin was a small café table and two chairs that served as their dining area. Six feet from each porch was a metal charcoal grill. The cabins weren't anything fancy, but they kept campers out of the elements, with an option for fireplace heat and electricity. None of the cabins had indoor plumbing. Guests needed to use the shower/bathroom houses along with those who stayed in their tents. Maybe one day we'd make enough to add plumbing and small bathrooms to each cabin along with a hotel-style heating unit, extending our season into the winter, but for now that wasn't a priority.

No, what was a priority was the body on the floor of cabin three.

I darted back outside and tied Elvis's leash to the front porch railing so I could better grip my cell phone in shaking hands.

"There's someone facedown on the floor," I told the emergency services operator. "They're over by the bed."

She sighed. Loudly. "Was there blood? A weapon? Are you sure he's not just taking a nap or passed-out drunk?"

"I can only see his legs from the door," I told her. "I didn't go in far enough to see more than that."

Another sigh. "Can you please go all the way in and check if he's not just snoring off a bender?"

I sucked in a surprised breath and stepped back inside the cabin. I hadn't thought about it just being a passed-out drunk. It would be horribly embarrassing to have called 911 on a not-dead person. Although, come to think of it, I really *would* like the police to come if someone had decided to move into one of the cabins and was sleeping off a binge.

"Well, he's on the floor and not in the bed, so I doubt he's just sleeping," I told the operator as I took a cautious step inside. "I'm assuming he would have heard me and woken up by now, but maybe he *is* drunk and passed out. Can you send the sheriff or a deputy anyway? I don't think I'm really capable of confronting a drunk and ousting him from my property."

"Check him first," she urged.

I was beginning to get angry at this woman. This was her *job*. This was the sheriff and deputy's job. Drunk or not, this person on the floor of cabin three was an intruder, and the law should come out here to help remove him and have me to file a report or something.

But I hated confrontation, so instead of insisting the operator send someone out right now, I tip-toed across the room. The man was facedown with one arm and part of his head hidden by the dust ruffle of the bed. What kind of person puts dust ruffles on a bed in a cabin? They just collect dust and make it harder to clean under the bed. And once they got dirty, the entire mattress needed to be yanked off to clean them and put them back. These things had to go even if they were a cute, blue gingham print.

Blood. There was a whole lot of blood. I stared down at it in panic, wondering if the man had gotten drunk, fallen, and hit his head or if he was truly dead. How much blood puddle-wise was a deadly amount to lose?

"Hello?"

"Yes, yes. I'm still here. There's blood on the floor, so I definitely think you need to send someone. It doesn't look like he's breathing. He kind of smells, but perhaps he hasn't showered in a few weeks, or maybe a rat died in the cabin or something. I don't want to touch him and mess up a potential crime scene."

Just like my mother, I too had watched many episodes of CSI, and while I clearly wasn't at Mom's level of confidence in proclaiming this man dead or estimating the time of death, I did know enough that I didn't want my prints and DNA all over anything.

And there was another reason why I didn't want to touch him. Death scared me. Death really scared me. I backed out of the cabin and stood on the porch, rubbing Elvis's ears for comfort.

"What's he look like?" the operator asked.

I held the phone away from my ear and stared at it in astonishment. "He's facedown. In fact, I'm not positive it's a man. He's kind of bulky and has dirty work clothes on and large boots, but some women are built that way."

The operator snorted. "Check him. I'm not sending Oliver or Sean out there for some drunk."

"Really?" I'll admit my tone was a little snappy. "Because I'd like to think my tax dollars pay for law enforcement to come out if a single, fifty-eight-year-old woman has a drunken vagrant trespassing on her property."

"It's probably just Dennis," she said, as if that was supposed to reassure me. "Len had to run him off a few times last year. He's harmless."

"Okay." I took a deep breath and walked back in. "Hey. You. Are you okay?" It sounded horrible, but I nudged the guy with my foot, not wanting to actually touch him.

"He's not responding," I told the operator. "If you don't want to bother the sheriff, then maybe send an ambulance?"

"Can you at *least* check if he has a pulse?"

The operator was irritated. That made two of us. The emergency services in this town were truly horrible. I hadn't had much opportunity to call for the police, or fire department, or even the ambulance in my life, but those few times when I had, this hadn't been my experience.

But I hated confrontation. *Hated* confrontation.

So I bent down to check the man. I just couldn't bring myself to touch the guy, though. Using my foot, I tried to roll him over, but he was too heavy. There wasn't anything nearby for me to use as a lever, so I put the phone on speaker, set it on top of the dresser, and reluctantly rolled the man over onto his back.

He flopped over. I let out an involuntary shriek and jumped back.

"He's dead. Oh, he's dead," I babbled.

The only deceased people I'd seen had been in caskets, carefully made up and arranged for viewing. None of those funerals has prepared me for this.

"Are you *sure?*" The woman sighed, as if I were some annoying window salesman calling in the middle of her dinner.

"Yes, I'm sure," I snapped, thinking that if the 911 operator were here, this wouldn't be the only dead body on the floor.

"Okay, I'll send Jake out," she told me.

I ran back out onto the porch, gulping fresh air and wondering who Jake was. She'd said Oliver and Sean earlier, so I'd assumed one of those was the sheriff and the other was the deputy.

But it didn't matter. I'd finally gotten this annoying 911 operator to do her darned job and send *someone* out to help me. Not wanting to deal with her any longer, I hung up the phone, sat down on the porch step with Elvis, and waited for the cavalry to arrive.

CHAPTER 3

The cavalry arrived in a battered, dark green Ford Super Duty diesel truck.

The man who stepped out wore blue jeans, a tan canvas jacket, and scuffed hiking boots. Silver-streaked hair peeked out from a green knit hat. He had a dark gray beard. It wasn't one of those sharp-edged beards worn by guys that hung out in coffee shops with their laptops, but it wasn't the wild, southern-rock-band kind of beard either. It was just a regular, medium length beard that looked like the guy trimmed every few weeks if he felt like it.

I stood up and plastered a smile on my face as he approached, thinking he might be a potential customer who was planning on some early spring hiking and had Googled nearby campgrounds. In a panic, I tried to think of how I could distract him before he got a close look at the state of the cabin porch, or caught sight of what lay inside.

Although he'd probably already seen the tree resting on the porch roof of cabin six. And the dilapidated sign at the entrance. And the potholes in the gravel drive.

"Yes, we're open." I beamed at him. "Are you looking for a cabin rental, or are you tenting it?"

He shot me a quizzical look, and I noticed his brown eyes were alert and intense. I squirmed, getting a feeling like I always did when a police officer was asking for my license and registration, or when I'd turned a paper in late in college. This guy was clearly judging me, seeing all the stuff I'd done wrong in my life and wondering whether he should give me a ticket or a failing grade.

"You called 911 about a dead body?" he asked.

So, not a potential camping customer then. I let out a breath, realizing that my police officer impression must have been right. But where was his uniform? His patrol car? His badge?

"You're Jake?" I asked, remembering the name the 911 operator had said before I'd hung up on her.

"Yeah." He waited. Expectantly.

I waited as well, then finally spoke. "Do you have a badge or something?"

"Not on me, no."

That was weird, but it was a Sunday, and from what the 911 operator had said, law enforcement seemed to take this day off. Still, I felt like I should do some sort of vetting here before I let him into the cabin.

"You're the deputy?" I motioned toward his coat pocket. "Do you have any ID at all?"

He dug around in his back pants pocket and produced a leather wallet. "I'm 'a' deputy, not 'the' deputy. Sometimes, anyway. When Oliver and Sean are busy, and I'm in the area of the problem, Shelly tends to call me."

Shelly must be the 911 operator's name.

"I live right up there on the mountain." He pointed behind himself at the foothill that rose up on the other side of the road from the campground, then handed me his license.

Jacob Irving Bailey. Rural Route 16, box 2, Reckless, Virginia. Six foot one. One hundred eighty-eight pounds. Fifty-nine years old. Capricorn. Organ donor.

I handed the license back after my long perusal. "I'm Sassy Letouroux. The body is in this cabin behind me—cabin three. Be careful on the porch. The floor boards need work and the railing is wobbly. And there's a hole in the roof. Not that the roof is going to fall on you or anything, but I thought I'd mention it. At least, I don't think the roof is going to fall."

He grunted, ignored my babbling, and went to move past me. Elvis blocked his path, slobbering on the guy's pants then turning around to beat the man with his tail. I worried for a second if dogs could be arrested for assaulting a police officer, but Jake just scratched the hound on his back, then went around him with a quick "good boy."

Elvis and I waited outside. Jake came out a few minutes later, his cell phone to his ear. He was barking out orders to someone, and once more I got that I'm-getting-a-ticket anxiety in the pit of my stomach.

Silly. You're not in trouble, I reassured myself.

A crunch of gravel on the drive drew my attention, and I turned around to see an ambulance slowly making its way down the potholed lane. The vehicle parked next to the green Ford, and a woman about my age jumped out.

Jake hit a button on his phone and shoved it back in his pocket. "Hey Steff," he called out to the woman. "I need the coroner, not the EMT."

"Gotcha." The woman spun around, but instead of getting back in the ambulance and driving off, she changed her jacket, swapping the navy blue for white one with a name embroidered in large black letters on the chest.

Stefanie Ostlund, Grant County Medical Examiner.

And the Town of Reckless EMT as well, evidently.

"Oliver here yet?" she asked as she snapped on a pair of latex gloves and grabbed a couple of shoe covers from the ambulance.

Jake snorted. "It's rib eye night at the Chat-n-Chew. He's out with the family, so you're stuck with me."

Stef rolled her eyes. "First dead body in years and our sheriff's too busy eating steak to show up. Remind me why I voted for him again?"

"'Cause he was the only one on the ticket." Jake gestured to me. "This is Sassy Letouroux, who I'm guessing is the new owner here. And her very handsome hound, who I have not yet been introduced to."

I nodded to Stef, not offering to shake her hand since she was already gloved up. "The bloodhound is Elvis. And my mother, Ellie Mae, is in the house getting a head start on the unpacking. She's actually the one who found the body."

"Nice to meet the pair of you." Stef nodded in return, then reached into the ambulance to pull out a duffle bag and a camera. "Now, if y'all'll excuse me, I've got a body to attend to."

She headed in. I saw the camera flash a few times through the cabin windows. Jake went to his truck and came back with a yellow legal pad of paper and a pen that had the end chewed off. I looked at the pen, wondering if he'd done the damage, or if he had a dog of his own. Elvis tended to destroy a pen with one chomp, so I was leaning toward Jake as the one with the gnawing habit.

"Can we go to the house?" he asked me. "I'll need to ask you and your mother a few questions for the report."

I nodded and led him over to the owner's house, Elvis on his leash beside me. The hound kept sneaking Jake adoring looks and making those low growling noises that meant he wanted your attention. Jake smiled down at him as we walked, scratching the hound's ears. By the time we walked inside, my bloodhound was glued to the man's side, nudging him for additional pets.

I unclipped Elvis's leash and offered Jake a chair at the dining room table. I could hear noise in one of the bedrooms, so I let Elvis off the leash, and headed back.

"Mom?" I poked my head into the smaller bedroom and saw her hanging up clothes and sorting through toiletries. "You can have the larger room, you know."

"I don't have much," she countered. "And with you sharing the room with Elvis, I figured you'd need more space."

True, but I still felt guilty. It didn't feel right for me to be in a bedroom nearly twice this size. But we could discuss that later.

"The deputy, or sometimes deputy, or whatever is here," I told her. "Jake Bailey. He needs to take our statements about the body in cabin three."

"Oh, of course!"

Mom dumped a handful of socks back into the box, then smoothed a hand over her hair before checking her lipstick in a compact mirror.

I wasn't sure if it was a generational thing or just differences in our personalities, but I'd never bothered much with the details of my personal appearance unless I was going on a date, to church, or to a special event. Mom never stepped outside without her hair done and her makeup on. Growing up, she'd always been completely coiffed and made-up before my brother and I even sat down for breakfast, but over the years she'd budged a bit from her hardline grooming standards. Nowadays she didn't do her hair or put on her makeup until after her first cup of coffee.

Mom followed me out of the bedroom and down the hall

to the main room, where I saw that Elvis had plopped himself down right next to Jake and was enjoying some ear scratches with his head on the man's knee.

"Jake, this is my mother, Ellie Mae Letouroux," I introduced them, not sure if I should call the man Deputy Bailey or by his first name. Did one address a temporary, occasional deputy with the title or without? I'd need to ask Mom later tonight, as she was my go-to on all things relating to etiquette.

Jake stood, much to Elvis's dismay, and removed his hat. "Ma'am. I'm sorry to disturb you, but I need to take a statement for the report."

Points for courtesy. He might be more than a little intimidating when he turned those brown eyes my way, but he had manners, and my dog liked him. That was good enough in my book.

"Of course." Mom moved over to the kitchen. "Can I get you some coffee? A muffin perhaps?"

Jake shook his head to say no, then his gaze landed on the gift basket. "Blueberry muffins? With Llama Land blueberries?"

I'd only been here for less than three hours, but I knew exactly what he meant. "Yep. Lottie Sinclair brought them over."

He smiled. "Then I *would* like one. And I'd appreciate a cup of coffee if it's no trouble, ma'am."

"It's no trouble at all." Mom waved at me. "Sassy, you give Mr. Bailey your statement while I get us all situated here. Cream and sugar, Mr. Bailey? Or is it Deputy Bailey?"

"Jake, please." He motioned me over to the table. "And just black, ma'am. Thank you."

He waited for me to sit, then lowered himself back into his chair. Elvis immediately resumed position, and Jake lifted his hand to stroke the dog, as if the limb were the blood-hound's to command.

"Tell me everything from the very beginning," he said.

I recited my tale from the moment Mom mentioned the dead body, to me looking for Elvis, then my ridiculously long conversation with the 911 operator.

"Is Shelly always like that?" I asked as Mom put out the coffee and muffins. It would be my second one in the last hour, but I certainly wasn't going to say no.

"We don't get a lot of emergencies in Reckless," Jake explained. "Celeste Crenshaw's repeatedly missing pig aside, the most excitement we've had in the last month has been when Lucky Miller got his hand caught in the soda vending machine trying to steal a Mountain Dew."

"I still think she should have been a little more helpful about a potential dead body," I groused.

Jake nodded. "Some of that is on account of you being a stranger here in Reckless. Some of that is because our sheriff hates missing out on a good rib eye dinner. Some of that is because Shelly probably couldn't believe that there actually was a dead body. But I'll have a word with her about her customer service skills if you like."

I bit my lip, thinking that as a stranger in town, I might not want to be getting into a pissing match with the 911 operator. That whole not liking confrontation thing rose again, and I shook my head.

"Never mind. I'm sure she was just having a bad day. There's no need to go getting anyone in trouble."

Especially not on my first day here.

Jake nodded in agreement, took a bite of his muffin, then made an appreciative noise.

"I was told the blueberries are so good people get into fights trying to buy them each year," I commented. "But

Lottie Sinclair is no slouch when it comes to baking. She should open a business—either a bakery, or if there already is one, maybe she can supply them with a few special items. Or run a cottage, custom-order bakery out of her home." I caught myself before I went too far into planning and organizing a business for a woman I'd just met not three hours ago. I had enough to do here at my campground without taking on any extra work.

"Lottie Sinclair is indeed a fine baker." Jake took another bite of the muffin, then set it down before turning to my mother. "Now Ms. Letouroux, why don't you tell me everything. Start with how you came upon the body in cabin three."

"Well, we'd just arrived and Sassy was getting things squared away with Elvis. I just get *so* excited, being in our new home and all, that I went on a short wander. You know —just to see the cabins, the layout, look at the lake and all that. I haven't been here in over forty years. We didn't get to see the place in person before we bought it, just the videos from the real estate agent, and like I told Sassy, those people just want to make a sale."

Jake blinked in surprise, then turned to me. "You bought the place sight unseen?"

Heat washed over my face at the accusation, but it wasn't like I hadn't worried over the same thing. "I used to come here as a kid, and I'd brought my son here a few times when he was little. It's not like I've never been here before. And we had our own buyer's agent, and an inspection…"

But yeah. Sight unseen. The price had been right, and I'd negotiated down from there, so I'd figured if there were a few scratches in the paint job that our agent had neglected to point out, we'd still be getting a good deal. I'd been busy wrapping things up at my job at the time and hadn't been up for the six-hour round trip. Mom couldn't drive for that long. I'd trusted in my agent, the home inspector, and in fate, and taken the plunge, investing my entire life savings in this place.

It seemed a reckless action, sitting here right now, but at the time, it had felt like a divine intervention, an opportunity for me to turn my life around, to realize a long-held dream, to take a risk and do something out of passion instead of responsibility.

Heck, the town was named Reckless. I guess that meant I fit right in.

"A few of the cabins looked like they needed some work." Mom went on. "I wanted to see how bad it was, so I picked one and walked in."

"They're supposed to be locked," I told Jake. "All the buildings. I haven't checked any of the others, but the owner's house was locked. Cabin three clearly wasn't."

"The cabin is very cute," Mom continued. "Just the sort of place where I would have loved to stay when I was younger and didn't have to worry about my back all the time. I walked in and saw a pair of legs on the other side of the bed—laying on the floor, you know. I went to see what had happened because it's not normal for someone to be lying on the floor when there's a perfectly good bed right there beside them."

Yet another difference between Mom and I. She'd waltzed right on up to what could have been a passed-out vagrant without a second thought where I'd hovered in the doorway wishing I'd brought some mace. Of course, I'd been told the person was dead and had a fear of death. Mom had probably assumed it was someone who might need medical aid.

"Can you describe exactly what you saw?" Jake tore a piece of paper out of his notepad and passed it over to Mom with a spare pen. "Or better yet, draw it for me?"

"Of course." Mom got to work, the tip of her tongue sticking out of her mouth the way it always did when she was concentrating. While she worked, Jake finished off the muffin and drank his coffee. I got up to get him a refill, and when I came back, Mom was pushing the drawing over to him.

"I warn you that I came close to failing art class in high school," she said.

"I'm sure it's fine, ma'am." Jake looked at the picture, clamping his mouth into a hard line. I knew he was trying not to smile, and I appreciated it. Mom was the first one to laugh at herself, but he didn't know that.

"Nice stick figure, Mom," I teased as I slid another cup of instant coffee to Jake, then grabbed a chocolate out of the gift basket for myself. "It's very much in the style of Picasso. I don't know why you doubt your artistic ability."

Mom snorted and swatted at me. "Picasso. Maybe I should have pursued an art career after all. I can draw lines and squares."

"That's more than I can do," I told her as I went back to my seat.

"Did you touch the body at all?" Jake asked as he stuffed the drawing into his notepad. "Check for a pulse? Move it so you could see the head or face?"

"Oh no. I've seen *all* the CSI shows. The *Law and Order* ones too. I saw that blood, didn't see the man's chest move at all, and knew he was dead. His head was under the bed and hidden by the dust ruffle, but I wasn't about to move him."

Jake scratched some notes. "Did you touch anything in the room? The light switch? Grab the bed post to steady yourself from the shock of finding a dead body?"

Mom sniffed. "I'm not the fainting, unsteady type. And the curtains were open as well as the door behind me. I could see well enough with the sunlight coming in that I didn't need to turn on the lights."

Jake nodded. "So then you came back here and told your daughter to call 911?"

I winced, not really wanting him to hear this part of the story, but just as mom wasn't the fainting, unsteady type, she also wasn't the lying type.

"Of course not. We had a guest. I told Sassy about the body after our guest had left." Mom thought for a second. "Actually it was a bit after our guest had left because I kind of forgot about it. But Elvis had gone missing and Sassy was frantic, thinking he'd be halfway across the state sniffing a rabbit or something. That's when I said that I hoped he wasn't over in cabin three messing with the dead body."

Jake set down his pen and put his head in his hands for a few seconds. Then he blew out a breath and looked up. "You forgot."

Mom shrugged. "I'm eighty-five. And we had a guest, so I got a little distracted. Hospitality is important, you know. We're new here and we're running a business. I didn't want the first visit with a neighbor to be sullied with something so unsettling as a dead body in one of our cabins. I told Sassy as soon as our guest had left. Well, as soon as I remembered after she left, that is."

"It was Lottie Sinclair," I interjected, wanting to turn the sometimes-deputy's attention from my mother's eccentricities to something else. "She got here as I was starting to get things out of the car. We went in, chatted, had some coffee and muffins from the gift basket she'd brought, then she left. She was only here for about an hour."

Jake sighed, rubbing his temple before continuing to write. "So your mother told you about the body in cabin three, and you called 911?"

I winced. "Well, not right away. Elvis was missing and I

needed to find him first." I felt a wave of defensiveness at the accusation in Jake's expression. "I wasn't sure if I'd heard my mother right or not and I was worried about my dog. He's never been here before and there are lots of interesting smells for him to track. He was alive, and if I'd heard my mother right, the body was dead. So I was focusing on my alive, missing dog. I was worried he'd wander into the road and get hit, or onto someone's land and get shot, or lick a poisoned toad, or drown in the lake or something."

"Your dog doesn't swim?" Jake looked down at Elvis, who was snoring away with his head still on the sometimes-deputy's knee.

"I don't know if he swims or not. He came from a rescue in Texas." Did they have lakes in Texas? Did Elvis have the opportunity to swim in one in his prior life there? I didn't know these things. I'd never been to Texas, and I envisioned the whole state as one giant desert with a few big cities springing up from the sand.

Jake sighed. "So you found your dog. Alive. Then you called 911?"

"Yes," I replied, glad to focus back on the matter at hand and not my mother's and my questionable priorities. "Honestly, you shouldn't be mad at mom and I for the delay in calling this in. That 911 operator took forever to send you out here," I pointed out.

He nodded. "Yes. I know. Is there anything else you need to add to the statement?"

Mom and I looked at each other and shook our heads.

"Good." Jake rose, giving Elvis an apologetic pat as he did. "I'll call if you need to come down to the station and give us your fingerprints, just in case they show up in the cabin somewhere. I know y'all said you didn't touch anything, but sometimes people forget."

I stood as well. "Fingerprints? Why? Was it...did he...I

thought the man was a vagrant, that he was drunk and fell and hit his head on something and died."

"He was murdered," Jake's voice was soft and full of sympathy as he glanced at my mother, then back at me. "And before I leave, I really think I should check the other cabins. Just to be on the safe side."

CHAPTER 4

"*M*urder?" I squeaked. Suddenly I really didn't want to be staying here tonight, alone with my eighty-five-year-old mother and a friendly bloodhound who would probably open the door to any intruder.

"I'm sure Daryl Butts's death had nothing to do with you ladies or the campground," Jake said.

I was *not* reassured. "How can you say that? The man was found dead in one of our cabins. The door was unlocked. Was he doing some sort of drug deals here, and his buyer or supplier offed him? Was he cheating on his wife with someone in the cabin, knowing the place was vacant, and an angry husband killed him? Was he a spy meeting his Russian contacts here, and they turned on him?"

My imagination was running wild, and I was honestly afraid for my mother and me.

"Now, just settle down." Jake made downward motions with his hands that did nothing to settle me, and a whole lot to annoy me. "Daryl might have been a drinker, but he wasn't into drugs and he wasn't a spy. And trust me, no woman within a hundred miles would get into bed with him. I doubt he's seen a naked woman since his wife left ten years ago."

None of that helped my fears. A *murdered man* had been found in one of my cabins. By my mother. Were the killers coming back? Was this a regular thing here in Reckless? I hadn't thought to check crime statistics before I'd put in an offer on the campground because I'd always remembered this as a sleepy small town and a beautiful vacation spot.

Wait. *Daryl*? Daryl Butts? The handyman?

Well, that might explain why the place was falling apart. Although judging from the CSI shows I'd watched, he hadn't been dead long enough to excuse the property's neglect.

"He was the campground's handyman," I stated. "And he was murdered here, in the campground, inside one of the cabins. How do you know the murderer won't be coming back?"

"*Why* would the murderer be coming back?" Jake shook his head. "Daryl's dead. There's no reason for his killer to come back."

I thought about that for a second. If Daryl drank and gambled, he probably owed someone money that wasn't getting paid, or had cheated at cards, or pissed the wrong person off. Daryl worked here. Everyone knew he worked here. He was probably murdered in one of the campground cabins because that's where the killer knew to find him.

I blew out a breath, feeling sorry for the guy. He'd most likely been here to fix the rickety porch, and the killer had accosted him. True, I hadn't seen any tools or even Daryl's vehicle, but the killer might have taken them as payment for the debt the dead man owed.

Suddenly I was spinning a whole crime documentary in my imagination. And that played out with the killer long gone, pawning tools and a stolen truck and never stepping foot in Reckless or my campground ever again.

"Okay," I said, feeling a bit better. "You're probably right."

Jake put a hand on my shoulder for a quick, reassuring squeeze. "I'll take a look around before I leave, and we'll make sure everything is locked up nice and tight, but I truly think this thing with Daryl had nothing to do with the campground. Len had felt sorry for the guy and hired him on years ago. There aren't a lot of handymen available in Reckless for hire. Len didn't exactly have his pick of applicants. Daryl came with a lot of baggage, and he wasn't what I'd call a reliable or conscientious employee. Let's just say there are a dozen people at least who would have wanted to see him dead, and none of their motives would have anything to do with you, your mother, or this campground."

I nodded. It sounded as if Daryl had some issues he'd been battling that weren't involved with drugs or being a spy or having an illicit affair. Gambling and alcohol addiction. The poor man. I felt ashamed at my irritation with Daryl and vowed to have more tolerance in the future. The man was dead. Murdered. I needed to be a whole lot less judgmental and more gracious.

"I'll be right back," I told mom as I grabbed the enormous ring of keys I'd received at closing this morning.

"I'll keep Elvis in the house," she replied. "And I'll keep unpacking. It'll be good to be settled in, even if we'll have to rearrange everything once the movers get here with the furniture tomorrow."

Jake and I headed out, walking in silence to the cabins on the other side of the owner's house. We started with number twelve. Jake waited patiently while I sorted through the keys, making a mental note to tag each one so I didn't have to go through this each time I needed to clean the cabins for a turnover.

I opened the door and Jake edged himself in front of me as he entered, waving for me to stay back. He finished his sweep with a "clear" pronouncement that made me wonder if he had at one point been more than a sometimes-deputy, or if he'd been military. I edged my way in, flicking on the light to check the electricity and giving cabin twelve a good once-over myself.

Same furnishings at cabin three. Three books on the nightstand. Same mid-century décor. I smiled, kind of liking the aesthetic at Reckless Camper Campground. I could work with this whole 1970s vibe. Maybe I'd make it a retro theme and market the heck out of it.

Exiting, I locked up before we walked to the next cabin. After we'd finished checking the nine cabins to the left of the owner's house, I'd realized a couple of things. One—Len Trout's wife had probably done the decorating fifty years ago and when she'd died, he'd not changed a thing. Two—Daryl Butts had been a lousy handyman.

No disrespect to the dead intended, and I was fully open to all sorts of reasons why this might have not been the man's fault, but the place was a mess. If Len had hired him out of sympathy, he must have suspected the guy wasn't up for the task. Nothing Jake and I saw was quite as bad as the tree on the roof of cabin six and the porch disaster of cabin three, but every single dwelling we entered showed signs of deferred maintenance. I had no idea what sort of filter our real estate agent had used on her camera when she'd videoed these cabins, but I hadn't seen the dirt, the rot, or the mold when I'd been considering what I should offer for the place.

I kept all these thoughts to myself, not wanting to voice them and have Jake reply that I shouldn't have bought a campground sight unseen. That water was long under the bridge, and I didn't need a sometimes-deputy I'd just met judging me.

I checked in on mom and Elvis before Jake and I made our way over to the three cabins on the other side of the owner's house. The rickety porch of cabin three was covered with yellow crime scene tape. I stopped to look at it for a few seconds.

"How long do you think you'll need to keep the tape up?" I asked.

"No more than a day. Two at most. It's up to the sheriff, but it's not a big cabin and both Stef and the techs should have gotten most of what they needed today."

I sighed, thinking of the campers who should be arriving next week, then felt like a callous jerk. A man had died. Been murdered. And I was worried I wouldn't have all twelve cabins to rent for the early hiking season. Heck, given the condition of at least two of them, the crime scene tape was the least of my worries. If I didn't manage to get the needed repairs done, I'd only have ten cabins to rent at best.

I did the math and chewed my lip in thought. We needed the April camper income to fund some improvements I'd wanted to make to the docks and the common areas. If we were lucky, a few of the RV regulars would arrive early, but the income from tent campers wouldn't really start coming in until early May, depending on the weather. Cabin rentals had the longest season and the most earnings potential, and I didn't want to have even one of them out of commission.

"I'll talk to the sheriff," Jake said as we continued walking. "It might be Sunday and rib eye dinner night at the Chat-n-Chew, but there's no reason he can't clear the scene by tomorrow afternoon at the latest."

I smiled at him in gratitude. "Thanks. I'll need to clean up inside. And fix the porch and the railing."

"Do you...are you...?" Jake looked over at me, his expression resembling a man about to cross a minefield. "I don't want to make assumptions or anything. Do you have carpentry experience? A background in home improvement or remodeling?" He glanced over at the fallen tree on top of cabin six. "Do you own a chainsaw?"

"No, no, and no." I nodded toward the garage. "There are saws and tools and mowers that came with the business. I haven't had time to really look at the entire inventory, let alone figure out if any of the mowers or saws even work. I'm willing to bet there's a chainsaw in there."

I'd never operated a chainsaw in my life, and quite honestly, was a little intimidated at the prospect. I'd absolutely tackle the porch repair with the help of some YouTube videos, but cutting up that tree was something I was definitely going to leave to someone who wasn't likely to cut her own arm off, or have the tree shift off the roof and on top of her.

"Put up a post on the Reckless Neighbor app for recommendations," Jake suggested. "I'll ask around as well. It won't be easy to find someone willing to do part-time or even full-time handyman work, but there's probably a few companies over in Derwood that would be able to come out. Make sure they give you a quote for specific repairs, though. I'd like to think we're all honest, small-town folk here, but some people try to take advantage of newcomers."

"Thanks," I told him. "That's a great idea, and I'll definitely get a few quotes." I'd try, at least. Time was the deciding factor here, and I might have to pay extra just to get these cabins fixed in the next week or two.

I was regretting that I'd told Lottie I'd go with her to the tourism board meeting tomorrow afternoon with all that I had to do. There were things Mom couldn't manage, and without a handyman, mowing, weed-eating, filling potholes in the driveway, and minor repairs would all fall on my shoulders. But I *really* needed to go to that meeting and begin to set up an events schedule for the camping season that complemented what was going on in town. I'd just have to pull some early mornings and long nights if I was going to have everything ready for our guests.

I walked up to cabin one and unlocked the door, immediately stepping aside for Jake to enter. We'd gotten a routine down, and were like a synchronized swimming team in how we approached each cabin at this point. At his "clear" I entered and looked around, my gaze immediately falling on the bedside table.

Two books. Not three. I frowned, wondering if there had been two or three books in cabin three. I hadn't really noticed since I'd been focused on the body on the floor. But all the other cabins had three books on the nightstand, and this one only had two. I wondered if I should point out this discrepancy to Jake or not. I quickly decided on no. He was a trained professional, and I wasn't. If the missing book in this cabin had been a clue, surely he would have picked up on it.

I thought about the hundreds of books in the owner's cabin and figured that occasionally a guest might take one home with them. If they hadn't finished the novel, or if they particularly loved it, I was sure it wouldn't have crossed some people's minds that taking a book from a rental cabin was stealing. Many places had those "take me" bookshelves, or free libraries. Some camper this past summer had probably stuck the third novel in his bag and not thought twice about it. Heck, for all I knew, Len had encouraged that practice.

So I kept my mouth shut, making a mental note to grab a random book off the wall of shelves in the owner's house and bring it over when I did my cleaning.

I locked up and we headed to cabin two. Finding nothing unusual inside, I locked that cabin as well and started to walk Jake back to cabin three where his truck was still parked.

"This way." He pivoted, taking my arm and heading back

to the owner's house. "I want to make sure you're safe inside before I leave."

It wasn't dark yet. Actually it was at least two hours until sunset. I eyed Jake nervously, my worries returning.

"Call me old-fashioned, but I escort a lady to her door," he grumbled. "This has nothing to do with the murder or your campground or your safety. It's just me being an old fart."

I hid a smile, relieved at his explanation. As promised, he walked me to the door, thanked me for mine and my mother's cooperation in this matter, then left. I went inside, but watched out the living room window until I saw his truck disappear down the drive.

"I like him," my mother's voice sounded behind me.

"Me too," I told her. "Me too."

CHAPTER 5

*M*om and I had planned for a first night without furniture or small appliances. In spite of the whole finding-a-dead-body thing, we were in a celebratory mood about our new venture and our new home. Rather than dive right in to the business end of things as Corporate Me wanted to do, we decided instead to just relax, enjoy the evening, and get settled in.

Mom opened the bottle of wine we'd packed while I fed Elvis and put some music on the little Bluetooth speaker I'd connected to my phone. While Mom started putting some sandwiches together for dinner, I grabbed my plastic cup of wine, hauled the air mattresses into the bedrooms, and got to inflating them. Starting in Mom's room, I got the mattress unboxed, then pulled out sheets and a blanket. She'd already unpacked her hanging clothes and had the folding ones sorted and ready to go in dresser drawers when the furniture arrived tomorrow. While the mattress inflated, I turned one of the empty boxes into a makeshift bedside table and put a towel over it. Her cell phone charger, pill bottle, and e-reader went on top. A flashlight went beside the bed, just in case the power went out and she couldn't find the flashlight app on her phone. After I made up her bed, I inflated the second mattress in my room, then decided to take a break and head back into the main room to eat.

Elvis had finished his dog food and was eyeing Mom's and my dinner with intent, so I put him in the enclosed back porch, making sure the deadbolt was thrown to the outside door. He stood at the sliding door to the porch, his nose pressed against the glass as he stared at us. A long line of drool hung from his jowls, and his deep-set eyes informed me from under their wrinkles that he hadn't eaten in weeks.

I'd just fed the dog, but he had a bottomless belly when it came to people-food. He also had a very tricky stomach when it came to human food, and him snatching a sandwich would mean I'd be putting up with eye-watering dog flatulence all night. Just as Elvis was a pro at opening doors, he was also a world-class thief when it came to food. He was tall enough to snatch most food off the counter without even jumping. I'd caught him standing on the table once, nosing open a box of pizza that I'd thought was safely in the center. He'd stolen more donuts than I'd probably eaten in my whole life. Even eggs and butter on the counters, warming to room temperature for baking, weren't safe. If you turned your back for a second, they were gone, shells and wrapper and all. Gone without a trace.

Trying to ignore my dog's silent begging, I sat at the table and surveyed what Mom had put together. She'd made turkey and swiss cheese sandwiches on multigrain bread with lettuce, tomato, and avocado. We were eating off paper plates, the chip bag open on the table. I dug into my sandwich, absolutely starved after our busy day.

In record time, we'd polished off our food and made a serious dent in the bag of chips. I leaned back in my chair, relaxed and enjoying the feeling of being in our new home.

"Chocolates and a wine refill? Mom asked as she gathered up the paper plates.

"That sounds lovely," I told her.

Mom cleaned up—which amounted to tossing our "dishes" and giving the counter a quick wipe with a paper towel. I stuck our garbage bag into one of the cabinets, safely away from Elvis, then let the bloodhound back in while Mom refilled the plastic wine cups and set out an assortment of chocolates from Lottie's gift basket.

We relaxed while Elvis sniffed around the table for any dropped crumbs. As I sipped my wine, I tried to envision how the room would look once our furniture arrived—and how the campground would look mowed, maintained, with flowers and cute seating areas, and fishing poles outside the office door waiting to be used. I knew this was going to be a lot of hard work, but it was also going to be fun—and so rewarding. No more eight AM conference calls. No more late-night meetings. I'd be up long before eight, and definitely working into the night, but it would be for *our* business. And I'd be in shorts and a tank top, not a business suit.

"Any ideas on activities for our first few weeks?" Mom asked, popping a chocolate into her mouth.

"Easter is coming up. It looks like the first round of guests arrive next Monday, so I was thinking of an egg-dying party on Wednesday. Each guest will get one egg to decorate however they choose. I want to think of something really fun to do on Friday, then maybe an egg hunt on Sunday. We could hide plastic eggs with individually wrapped candies in them."

"You could repeat the activities the following week," Mom pointed out. "I'll check but I'm pretty sure those first reservations are only for one week, so it would be all new guests."

I nodded. "Maybe I'll repeat a few activities in the beginning, but I'd like to eventually do something different each week."

It would be a lot of work coming up with twenty-five to thirty unique activities, but I wanted to give the local campers an incentive to come more than once a season—and the out-of-state folks a good reason to come back. Hiking. Fishing. Canoeing and Kayaking. Bird watching. And fun activities for the whole family.

"Friday night is going to be the highlight of the week," I mused. "Themed parties, food, and contests."

"Sounds good." Mom looked at her watch. "It's not even nine o'clock yet. What should we do? Without a television, I'm a bit lost."

"We have internet," I said, thankful that I'd made arrangements for the transfer of electricity and internet service before closing. "We could stream a movie on my tablet. Or we could read."

I gestured to the wall of bookshelves. Mom chuckled, then got up and went to look at the books.

"Heavens, there's hundreds of them here." She pulled one off the shelf and pointed at the spot. "Look, there's another row behind these. We won't lack for reading material—at least not for the next few years."

I got up to join her, thinking there probably wouldn't be many books here I'd be interested in reading. I was a picky reader. I liked science fiction, romance, and mysteries, but that was about it. Glancing over the titles, I realized a most of the books were non-fiction, and the few fiction ones looked to be classics.

Mom showed me the one she'd taken off the shelf. "A History of Haberdashery in the Nineteenth and early Twentieth Centuries."

"Hopefully it's illustrated." I took one off the shelf as well and turned it to show her. "Hummingbird Migration Patterns from 1950 to 1960."

"Len Trout certainly had an odd taste in reading material," Mom said as she put the book back on the shelf.

I did the same. "Maybe these were his wife's?"

Mom snorted. "And not a romance among them? I doubt it."

"Okay, so maybe she wore the romance books out, and these are the ones she barely opened." I pulled another book out, looking at the first few pages. "They're all really old. I wonder if they're worth anything?"

"Probably worth as much as that couch," Mom drawled. "Once I get time, I'll box them up and see if there's anywhere in town that takes used books. Maybe the library will want them?"

"Or the senior center," I suggested.

Mom shook her head. "Just because we're old doesn't mean we want to read about hat fashion a hundred years ago."

"Someone might," I said. There were plenty of birdwatchers who might be thrilled to find that hummingbird book, and probably history buffs who might be intrigued by the hat one. I thought of Lottie's son, who was studying history in college, and wondered what exactly his specialty was. I'd try to remember to ask her tomorrow, so I could keep an eye out for history books he might like when we eventually sorted through them all.

Giving up on the books, I took Elvis for one last walk, then Mom and I ended up streaming a movie until bedtime. I walked into my room, ready to throw the sheets on my air mattress and get a good night's rest, only to find the thing flat on the floor.

"Darn it." I knelt down and checked to make sure I hadn't accidentally left the valve open. It was sealed tight. When I pushed down on the deflated mattress, I heard the hiss of air coming from one of the seams. Great. The mattress had a leak. At least Mom's was okay.

Elvis came into the room to stand beside me. We both looked down at the saggy mattress.

"Well, buddy, we've got a choice here," I told the dog. "We can blow this thing up again and have it flat within a few hours at best. Or we can sleep on the sofa."

The dog looked up at me, then walked out of the room.

"Good choice," I muttered.

I really didn't want to sleep on that ratty old sofa, but it really was the better option. Grabbing the bedsheets and blanket, I did my best to turn the floral monstrosity into a decent sleeping area. It squeaked as I lay down, and I shifted around a bit to evade a spring that wanted to poke me in the back. Elvis hopped up and curled into a ball at my feet. It meant I'd have to sleep the night with my legs bent, but I didn't have the heart to deny my dog a portion of the couch. He'd slept on my bed since the day I'd brought him home, and I didn't have anything else he could use. I wasn't about to make him sleep the night on the hardwood floors.

Elvis shifted a little, resting his head on my leg. I stretched to turn off the light, being careful not to disturb him. Then I closed my eyes and, in spite of the uncomfortable sofa, fell right to sleep.

* * *

I WOKE IN THE DARK, confused as to where I was and what woke me. Blinking a few times to clear the sleep, I remembered that I was in my new house at the campground and not the townhome I'd lived in for the last twenty years. The kitchen came into focus, barely visible with the dim glow of the hallway nightlight. I heard a low growl and realized that was what had awakened me. Elvis was no longer on the couch at my feet, but standing at the window by the dining room table, staring intently into the dark. His tail was high, curled almost over his back. His floppy ears were forward. His silhouette absolutely still at the window, he gave another low growl.

I shivered, suddenly afraid. Elvis was a lover, not a fighter. And he explored his world through his nose. Unlike the border collies he'd played with at the dog park, a deer could run right across Elvis's path, and he wouldn't chase after the bounding animal. No, Elvis would drop his head to the ground, start sniffing, and track the deer through the woods, but he wasn't enticed by movement.

That was what made his stance and that low growl so alarming.

I wanted to bury my head under the blanket and hide, but I was a grown woman, so I got up and padded over to the window, resting a hand on Elvis's head as I peered out.

"What do you see, boy?" I whispered. "Or is it something you hear?"

His tail wagged in a giant circle and he looked up at me. Reassured, I patted his head and kept looking. Maybe it had been a rabbit or a raccoon or something. A bear, or deer. Elvis never seemed bothered by the squirrels back home, but the presence of a new, unknown animal might have spooked him.

I didn't see or hear anything, but something made me remain at the window just a little bit longer. That's when I saw a faint light over near one of the cabins—or maybe it was *in* the cabin.

I squinted, wondering if it had been a trick of the moonlight or my imagination. It hadn't been very bright, like a flashlight bobbing around or anything. It had been dim. Like light reflecting off something. Or like a tiny penlight.

There. I saw it again. My heart speeded up as I realized that the faint flash of light was over near cabin five...or perhaps cabin eight. No, it was cabin five. Biting my lip, I wondered what I should do. I didn't own any sort of weapon, and even if I had, I wouldn't have wanted to go running out there and accidentally shoot out the window of a cabin, or kill some innocent animal. I looked down at Elvis, who'd given up his guard-dog impression and had returned to the tail-wagging slobber-monster I knew and loved. He wasn't an attack dog, and while a hound his size might scare off an intruder, I didn't want to take the risk that Elvis might get shot himself.

I glanced back at Mom's bedroom, not wanting to wake and worry her. I'd seen enough crime shows in my lifetime that I did write her a quick note, letting her know that I was going out to check on a light over near cabin five. That done, I threw on my coat, hooked Elvis's leash on him, and grabbed the ring of keys, lacing a few of them through my fingers. I'd walked through many a parking lot at night with my keys held this way, in hopes that if I was ever attacked, I could use them to poke out my assailant's eyes or at least scratch him up. And just as I'd done so many times in the past, I sent up a quick prayer that I wouldn't need them.

As soon as we were out the door, Elvis practically dragged me down the porch steps and over to the row of cabins where I'd seen the light. I really wanted to take a stealthier approach, but maybe whatever or whoever it was would hear us coming and take off.

Right at the edge of the garage Elvis stopped so suddenly that I nearly fell over him. The fur on his back rose, and he stared at cabin five.

My breath came shallow and quick. I was gripping the keys so hard that I'd probably have indentations in my fingers for a week.

I should have gone back and called 911, but I didn't want to have to deal with that Shelly telling me to go check it out myself before she bothered any of the local law enforcement. Plus, I owned this campground now. It was mine, and I didn't need to be calling the police every time I heard a noise or saw a light. I'd be the laughingstock of Reckless if I freaked out every time a raccoon or bear got into the garbage, or a bird hopped around with something shiny and reflective in its beak.

When this was over, I was getting a gun. Not a real gun. Something like a BB gun, or one of those air-pellet things. Or maybe a shotgun I could load up with the little stuff. I didn't want to actually shoot something, just to fire it off and maybe scare whatever it was away.

Before I could lament my lack of weaponry any longer, Elvis let out a long, low bay.

I loved my hound's song. Those deep crooning bays coming from the depths of his chest always brought a smile to my face. This didn't bring a smile to my face. I was pretty sure this was the noise escaped convicts heard right before a pack of bloodhounds took them down.

The moon went behind a cloud, but just before it did, I saw a shadow stir on the porch of cabin five. Elvis bayed again and leapt forward, nearly yanking me to the ground. I dug in my heels and held him back, not wanting my dog to rush headlong into a fight with a bear. Or a man. Or a man-bear. At this time of night, out here near the woods, I wasn't ruling man-bear out.

The moon broke free. Elvis was baying and straining at the leash, but now he was facing toward the woods, and not the cabin. I debated getting out my cell phone to turn on the flashlight app, but decided I'd rather have the keys in my hand instead. Although if I was going to have to face a bear, at least the flashlight might blind him. The keys wouldn't do one bit of good.

Slowly I edged my way forward, making no attempt to shush Elvis. Whatever was out here had hopefully been spooked away at the dog's first bay, but his continued ruckus wouldn't hurt if the man, bear, or man-bear had any thoughts of returning.

By the time I reached cabin five, my ferocious monster of a dog had settled down and begun to sniff his way up the porch. I followed, leash tight in one hand, keys tight in the other. There was no sign of anything on the porch—nothing broken, no porch rails clawed or gnawed, no garbage or broken items strewn about. I let Elvis take a good sniff, watching as he made his way to the door. Sitting, he pawed at it.

I loosened my death grip on the keys, but didn't need to. Not only was the door not locked, it wasn't even closed all the way. I remembered the shadow I'd seen and wondered if the intruder had fled from inside, not worrying about closing the door in his haste to get away. Had it been an animal, searching for some leftover food? Had the dim flash of light I'd seen been some reflection as it moved around the cabin, knocking lamps and mirrors askew? I'd definitely closed and locked up every cabin when Jake and I had done our walk-through, but these doors were old. Maybe the lock bolt had slipped loose in the cold of the night.

I didn't want to think about the intruder being a person. Because if that was the case, not only was there possibly another set of keys floating around somewhere, but Jake was wrong and Daryl Butts's murder *did* have something to do with the campground.

"Bear, bear, bear," I chanted as I swung open the door. It was a sad state of affairs when my cornering a black bear was the best of two scenarios.

I flicked on the lights, jumping to the side of the door just in case some large animal or human wanted to run past me to get out. My eyes adjusted to the light, and I realized there was no one in the cabin except me and Elvis. Dropping the leash, I watched my dog sniff every inch of the cabin floor as I looked around. Nothing was tipped over or broken. It didn't look like someone or something had been searching the room for food or whatever. But as I bent to pick up Elvis's leash, I noticed that the mattress was slightly askew, and that there was a crumpled piece of paper next to the nightstand. It might have been here when Jake and I had checked the cabin, but just in case, I picked up the scrap of paper and stuck it in my jeans pocket.

Then I grabbed Elvis's leash, turned off the light, and securely locked the door. Once I'd gotten back in the house, I locked up and wedged a dining room chair under the front door knob, before curling up with Elvis on the couch for a sleepless night.

CHAPTER 6

*R*eckless Neighbors:
  The Easter Bunny will be making the rounds next Saturday and Sunday between the hours of two and four, riding on the Volunteer Fire Department ladder truck. For information on routes, check the Reckless Emergency Services website.

  Pickleball teams! We still need six more members for this summer's season. Sign up now at the Community Center, and get three alewives for free.

Alewives? I stared at the listing, imagining three stocky, middle-aged women dressed as if they were serving pints at a Renaissance fair. It was a weird thing to offer in return for signing up to play pickleball. Six team members meant the organizers were giving away eighteen alewives. Were there eighteen alewives in Reckless? That seemed like an excessive number of alewives for a town this size.

I'd hauled myself off my couch-bed at six in the morning, sleep deprived but giving up on getting any further rest. Tiptoeing around the house, I put water on to boil for the instant coffee, and took Elvis for a morning stroll. Our walk was longer than usual because I stopped by every one of the cabins, checking to make sure they were locked. Then I went inside cabin five once more, hoping that in the early morning light I could find some clue as to who—or what—had been inside last night. There were no footprints, no stray bear hairs, no dropped driver's licenses. Nothing to enlighten me any more than I had been last night. Deciding to blame the whole thing on a curious bear and a door that I'd somehow neglected to lock properly when Jake and I had made the rounds, I resolved to not waste any more time worrying about it. Tugging on the door to make sure it was locked tight, Elvis and I headed back to the house where coffee and fruit from Lotti's gift basket awaited.

As I made my instant coffee, I gave thanks that the movers would be here today and we'd be able to actually brew some decent stuff. Then I sat down with a paper bowl full of melon balls and pineapple slices, and checked the computer once more. This time I eyed the upcoming reservations for cabins, then clicked the tab to go back to the Reckless Neighbors app. There, I put up my first post asking for recommendations for someone who could cut up a fallen tree, and someone who could do repairs on a roof and a porch.

It felt a bit callous to be replacing Daryl Butts not twenty-four hours since Mom had discovered him dead in one of our cabins, but I needed those cabins fixed, and I didn't have the skill to do it myself. After the urgently needed repairs were done, I'd have to find someone to hire to do regular handyman work around the campground, but my priority right now was those two cabins.

Deciding I should do something besides fret about porch and roof repairs, I gathered together a bucket of cleaning supplies. Lottie would be here at one to take me to the meeting in town, but we had reservations coming up in a week, and these cabins weren't going to clean themselves.

Filling my Styrofoam cup with more coffee, I told Elvis to be good, left a note for Mom, and headed out to start cleaning.

Luckily the cabins didn't have indoor plumbing and I didn't have twelve bathrooms to clean. There were still the shower buildings with restrooms that would need a good scrubbing, but I'd take that any day over twelve individual bathrooms.

Starting with cabin one, I stripped off the linen and the comforters, and grabbed the pillows, putting everything in a pile on the porch. Then I scrubbed, polished, and cleaned. Once done, I dragged everything to the campground laundromat, threw it all into the three washing machines, then went back to start on cabin two. I cleaned quicker than the washers, so by ten o'clock I had a small pile of laundry waiting, but there were three cabins sparkling clean and ready to rent. I'd put the clean bedding on the day the guests were to arrive, in the meantime keeping it all clean and neat inside one of the closets in the house.

Mom was up by that point, scolding me for not waking her earlier. She joined me, taking over the laundromat duty and folding the clean linens once they were dry. I kept mopping, dusting, and polishing, trying to get at least two more cabins done before I needed to leave.

At noon I glanced at my watch, knowing I needed to hustle to get ready for the meeting. Mom took over, arguing that at eighty-five, she could still mop a darned floor without stroking out, and shooing me back to the owner's house.

I showered, then perused my wardrobe choices. One of the joys of my new life as campground owner was that I could dress in jeans or shorts and not have to wear a suit like I'd done for over thirty years of my life. But here I stood, staring at my closet, contemplating putting the dreaded suit on once more. With a sigh, I grabbed the outfit I'd hoped to never wear again, and dressed, somehow managing to slap on makeup and take Elvis outside by the time Lottie pulled down the drive in a BMW.

I did a double-take at the vehicle, not having pictured Lottie as the sort to be driving a luxury sedan. Putting Elvis back in the house, I waved and jogged down to meet her. She hopped out of the car and gave me a quick up-and-down glance.

Yeah. A suit. An olive-green pantsuit with a cream pin-striped tank top. I'd figured it was never too soon to make a good first impression and from Lotti's approving nod, I had. The suit plus the tan wool coat over top made me look as if I'd stepped right out of corporate America. As much as I'd preferred to go in jeans and a T-shirt, I wanted to make it clear to everyone in town that I was serious about making a success out of Reckless Camper Campground.

"Nice outfit. I feel a bit underdressed." Lottie smoothed a hand over her royal blue knee-length puffy parka.

Hardly. I was beginning to wonder if my new friend even owned a pair of jeans, or anything at all that wasn't brightly colored and perfectly coordinated. Underneath her coat Lottie had on a bright coral floral print dress paired with black, knee-high boots, everything accented with gold dangling jewelry. Her '80s hair was poofed out to the max, and her winged eyeliner brought me straight back to the sixties. Next to her I felt mannish with my understated makeup and my super short hair. Not that I could help the hair. It was finally growing back, and had at least gotten to the point where I'd managed to even it up. But my silvery blonde locks still weren't quite an inch long. There were days when I missed my long hair, but this was a whole lot easier to maintain and dried in about fifteen minutes without even needing a blow-dryer, so that was a plus.

"You look wonderful," I told her with all honesty. "I wish I could do my makeup like that." There were probably some

YouTube videos that could show me how, but in the last couple of years, I'd barely had time for cosmetics at all, let alone video tutorials.

"I'll come over one night and we'll have a makeup party," she promised. "Wine. All the eyeshadow and liner. Pizza. Movies."

"Strippers," I teased, unable to help myself.

Her eyes grew wide, and I suddenly wondered if I'd crossed a line. Then she laughed. "Oh, honey. There isn't a man in Reckless I'd be willing to waste a dollar bill on."

I grinned, hoping that she felt her husband was at least worth a dollar. But what did I know? I'd divorced over two decades ago and given up dating soon after. Maybe Lottie and her husband were long past passion and desire. Or not. It really wasn't any of my business.

I got into the BMW and Lottie flicked on the seat heaters. Sinking into the luxurious leather seats, I absorbed the scenery as she drove. Savage Lake seemed to have become incredibly popular over the last few decades. The houses around the campground were ones that had been here for generations, but as soon as we'd gone a few miles, new condos began to dot the shoreline as well as a few sprawling mansions. Glancing across the lake, I saw the same on the Savage side of the water. The lake was surrounded by four townships, all part of Grant County—Reckless, Savage, Derwood, and Red Run. Of the four, Reckless and Savage were the oldest, with Derwood the most populous and home to the large, big-box stores and supermarkets.

Once Lottie pulled into downtown Reckless, I started to recognize businesses from when I'd camped here years ago with Colter. The hardware store. The Chat-n-Chew. Bait and Beer. The courthouse. The old deli was now The Coffee Dog. The diner had changed hands and was now called Ruby's

Place. We drove past the library, and I remembered something I'd wanted to ask Lottie.

"You said your son, Aaron, was studying history in college?" I waited for her nod. "There are literally hundreds of old books that Len Trout's sons left behind in the house. A lot of them are history books, and I wondered if he'd be interested in some of them."

She wrinkled her nose. "Probably not. He reads everything on his e-reader now, it seems. Unless they're textbooks? Those things are hundreds of dollars each new."

Drat. I'd been hoping I could unload some of the books without needing to box them up and haul them somewhere.

"No, I didn't see any textbooks." I told her about the haberdashery one, and those I'd seen on local history. "There's a lot of naturalist books as well," I added.

"The library might want them," she told me as she turned into the parking lot behind the Community Center. "Or you could try Stumpy's Antiques and Oddities. Stumpy makes the flea market circuit in the summers, and I think I've seen him selling books."

I thanked her, making a quick note in my phone to check out Stumpy's when I had a chance.

We parked and walked into the community center, signing our names in an attendance book and sitting on folding metal chairs so hard that I wished I'd brought a cushion. There were about a dozen other people in attendance. A woman stood up on a makeshift stage behind a podium. She was tall and thin, as if she'd been stretched like taffy. Long legs. Long arms. Long torso. Narrow hips and shoulders. As the woman glanced up, I noted that even her face was long and thin, with a beak of a nose.

"That's The Bird," Lottie whispered to me.

Never had a nickname been so fitting. "Is she the mayor?" I whispered back. "County commissioner? Town Council?"

"Head of the Town Council." Lottie nodded toward the woman. "President of the Reckless Neighbors' Association, president of the town Ladies' Auxiliary, President of the Reckless Historical Society, and a member of the Savage Lake Events Committee."

Holy cow. Did the woman sleep at night?

"A *member* of the Savage Lake Events Committee?" I wondered. "Not the president?"

Lottie shushed me and shot an anxious glance toward the stage. "That's a sore subject. She lost out to Melinda Bakersfield. It was one more reason we've got an ongoing feud with the town of Savage."

The feud between the towns had probably been going on long before Melinda Bakersfield had been alive. Probably before The Bird had been alive, although in all honesty I got the impression she was the Methuselah of Virginia and had probably been running things since Jamestown.

At exactly half past the hour, The Bird called the meeting to order with a hearty whack of a crab mallet on the podium. For the next twenty minutes I took frantic notes while the woman went over all the events planned for the summer. She stressed how important it was that Reckless pull out all the stops for these events so that we could draw tourism traffic from the other towns. I hid an eyeroll, thinking the goal should be to increase tourism to the lake overall, with the whole making-Reckless-number-one secondary, but I was a newcomer here so I kept my mouth shut.

She wrapped up the meeting by announcing that the forms detailing each business's plans for each summer even were due by the end of next week.

Then she focused her raptor gaze on me. "You. You are Sassafrass Letouroux, the new owner of Reckless Camper Campground."

I gulped. "Yes, ma'am. My mother Ellie Mae and I arrived yesterday."

She nodded. "I'm glad to see you here this afternoon. It means you've got your priorities straight. Your form is due at the end of *this* week. That will give me time to mark it up and get it back to you in time for you to revise it and turn it in on time."

This week. That gave me only four days to come up with a detailed plan for how the campground would participate in these fourteen festivals. I'd absolutely intended on putting together a plan, just not so soon—especially not when cabins needed repairs and cleaning.

But I got the feeling no was not an answer The Bird would accept.

I sat up straight on the hard metal chair. "Yes, ma'am."

"She uses a red pen," Lottie whispered to me.

"Was she a school teacher?" I whispered back, thinking that The Bird probably taught school in 1684.

"Do you have something to contribute to this discussion, Lottie Sinclair?" The Bird snapped.

My eyes widened, and I focused on my notepad, cowardly abandoning my new friend to the wrath of this woman.

"Yes, I do have a question," Lottie bravely asked, her voice not even quavering. "Daryl Butts usually hangs the festival banners and the lights in the downtown trees. Now that he's dead, we need to assign that task to someone else."

The room fell eerily silent. I wasn't particularly surprised that Lottie knew the man had died less than twenty-four hours after I'd called it in, but I *was* surprised that no one else seemed to know. In a small town like this, I'd expected that gossip would spread fast—especially since it was a suspicious death.

I wasn't ready to call it a murder. If I did, I might not be able to ever sleep at night.

The Bird quickly got over her shock and shrugged. "I'll have Jake Bailey take over that task."

Lottie snorted. "Good luck with that," she muttered under her breath.

I hid a smile, thinking she was right. I got the impression that Jake wasn't the sort to be bullied into something by The Bird. Or by anyone. This woman might need to look elsewhere for someone to hang the banners and lights.

"How did you know Daryl Butts was dead?" I asked Lottie as The Bird turned her terrifying attention to another attendee.

"I heard Shelly call Jake to the campground for a medical emergency. I was worried about you and your mother, so I got on the roof with my binoculars."

"What?" I shot a quick glance at The Bird, then lowered my voice. "On the *roof*? With *binoculars*?" I didn't know what was more disturbing—that Lottie had been perched on top of her roof, that she was spying on my campground with binoculars, or that both those things seemed commonplace for her.

"It's a widow's walk the architect put in when Scotty and I built the house. Adds to the visual aesthetics or something." She waved a hand. "So it's not *really* the roof."

"I'm so relieved," I drawled.

"Anyway, I saw you and Jake by cabin three, so I knew you were okay, but I was still worried about your mother. Then when I saw Stefanie Ostlund change her jacket into the coroner one, I *really* got worried. That's when I went and got the high-powered rifle scope so I could get a good look inside the cabin window. As soon as I saw those big clunky work boots sprawled out on the floor by the bed, I knew it wasn't your mother. No self-respecting woman would wear boots like that, even if they had really big feet. And I know your mother doesn't have really big feet or such poor taste in footwear."

"No, she doesn't," I agreed weakly. Binoculars were bad enough, but *rifle scope*? Did I need to worry about Lottie snipering campground guests?

"I figured the only person who'd be dead on the floor of cabin three, or even at the campground at all, would be Daryl Butts. Just to make sure, I called a friend at the county morgue this morning to confirm." She shot me a curious look. "What did he die from? Heart attack? Alcohol poisoning? Tripped and hit his head on the bedpost?"

I held up my hands, feigning ignorance. "I really don't know. I guess Stefanie Ostlund will announce it when she determines a cause of death."

Lottie sniffed. "She'll let the police know, not us. Stef is notoriously closemouthed when it comes to these things."

"Well, hopefully someone will let me know," I fretted. "A man died in one of my cabins. One of my employees. Well, he would have been my employee if he hadn't died before I got there. How long had he worked for Len Trout? Maybe I should put up a plaque or a memorial tree or to honor the man."

It seemed like the right thing to do, but Lottie snorted in response.

"There's no need to memorialize that guy," she told me. "Daryl Butts wasn't a model employee. He wasn't a model anything."

That seemed kind of sad. Even bad handymen shouldn't die without anyone caring. Regardless of what Lottie said, I still felt a plaque or a tree mentioning his passing would be proper etiquette.

"Moving on," The Bird announced loudly. "We will now address matters having to do with the Reckless Historical Society."

No one budged from their chairs. I glanced over to Lottie, wondering if we really had to stay for this or not. She gave me a subtle head shake, and I settled in, a bit bummed that I couldn't get back to cleaning cabins.

The Bird removed a pin from her lapel, then replaced it with another pin. She stashed the crab mallet under the podium, then pulled out another one that looked identical to the first. With a quick rap, she called the second meeting to order. I listened with a half an ear, taking the opportunity to jot down some ideas for how the campground could participate in the summer festivals. If I couldn't be cleaning and prepping cabins, at least I could be planning.

The Bird finally adjourned the meeting. I was starting to rise from my seat when Lottie pulled me back down. "You gotta stay for the count," she warned me. "There's no Ladies' Auxiliary meeting today, thankfully, but there's the Neighbors Association one."

I sighed and watched as The Bird changed out her pin and crab mallet once more. It was near four o'clock when we finally filed out of the Community Center and into the parking lot. I was anxious over everything I still needed to get done today. I'd been gone so long, and hated that I'd left Mom to deal with the laundry, the unpacking, and the movers in my absence.

And I was hungry. That fruit I'd grabbed early this morning was long gone.

"Do you want to grab dinner?" Lottie asked as if she'd read my mind. "The Chat-n-Chew has an early-bird discount until four thirty. If we hustle, we can get chicken fried steak for fifteen percent off."

My stomach growled in approval at that idea, but I declined the offer, giving Lottie an apologetic smile.

"I need to get back," I told her, thinking that when I'd left at one o'clock for an events committee meeting, I hadn't expected to be gone for three hours. "Maybe next time when I don't have cabins to clean and prep, and movers arriving."

"Plus your plans for the summer festival are due on Friday." She smiled in return. "If you need any help with that, let me know. Len kept pretty good records of everything he'd done over the years for the festivals, but you'll probably want to step things up a notch. I'm happy to help brainstorm over a bottle of wine."

"I'm going to definitely take you up on that," I told her, thinking that maybe I could spare a few hours this week for some wine-and-planning with my new neighbor and friend.

A friend who climbed up on her roof to spy on the campground with a freaking rifle scope. But I liked Lottie. We all had our eccentricities, and she'd been so helpful, friendly, and welcoming, that I was willing to overlook the rooftop spying thing.

CHAPTER 7

I stood in front of cabin six, staring in amazement. While I'd been gone with Lottie, someone had not only sawed the fallen tree into a neat pile of logs, but they'd spread a tarp over the damaged portion of the roof and secured it. The smaller branches had even been cut up, stripped of their leaves, and bundled into kindling. Judging from the logs, the kindling piles, and the lack of leaves, whoever had done this had taken over half of everything with them—and all of the leaves. I didn't begrudge my fairy grounds-maintenance person that, and honestly would have let them have the whole lot.

I couldn't envision my eighty-five-year-old mother climbing up a ladder and sawing a tree, even if she'd managed to find a chainsaw somewhere, but I couldn't think of who else might have done it. Had someone in town felt sorry for my plight, knowing that my maintenance person had died? Was this the work of Jake, the sometimes-deputy? Or had Lottie sent her husband or a friend over and neglected to mention it?

Whoever it was, I hoped they'd left a bill with Mom. This

was a lot of work in return for some firewood. If I didn't owe them payment for the job, then I definitely owed them dinner and a huge favor.

Leaving the cabin, I went into the house, hoping Mom could shed some light on the mystery. She was at the computer, lists and schedules pinned to the wall beside the desk.

I immediately noticed that the battered dining room table and old floral-print sofa were still there—and our furniture was not.

"No movers yet?" I asked.

She shook her head. "I called and left a message, but they haven't gotten back to me."

I sighed, shifting my bedding aside to sit on the couch. Elvis hopped up to sit beside me and I rubbed his ears. The movers were probably on their way. Hopefully they'd get here soon so at least Mom and I could get the beds set up and wouldn't need to spend another night on an air mattress—or in my case, on the couch.

"What happened to your air mattress?" Mom asked. "I saw the bedding out here. Surely that couch couldn't have been more comfortable."

"Mine's got a leak," I confessed. "The couch was more comfortable than the floor." In reality it was probably only a smidgen more comfortable than the floor.

"Oh, honey. There's room on my mattress for the two of us," she suggested.

I shook my head. "There's not enough room for the two of us and Elvis. It's fine. One night on the couch isn't going to kill me."

"A night on that couch would probably kill *me*." Mom she leaned back in her chair. "How was the meeting? I finished the laundry, then came in here to check the reservations. I changed all the passwords and wrote the new ones down for you. I figured it was best to be safe since we didn't know who Len gave them to. Oh, and we've got five cabins booked for *this week* as well as three RV spots—all arriving Thursday. I didn't realize we'd be getting quite this many guests so early in the season."

Excitement fought with panic. Thursday. We were going to have our first guests in three days. There was so much to be done by then—mowing, cleaning, the potholes in the driveway, sprucing the place up so it didn't look like the former owner had died six months ago and no one had touched it since.

I took a few deep breaths and tried to think things through. With another day of cleaning, ten cabins would be ready to go. I was fairly certain the RV pads and hook-ups wouldn't require more than a quick check for plumbing and electricity. We could accommodate these guests, no problem. And this would give us some much-needed cash to do the repairs on cabins three and six, plus maintenance on the docks.

Which reminded me…

"Who cut up that tree that fell on cabin six?" I asked as I walked over to see what Mom had hung on the wall.

"That nice sometimes-deputy. Jake. He came by not five minutes after you left and offered to cut up the tree if he could have the logs. Seems his furnace burns wood, and according to him, it was a nice oak."

I wondered why he hadn't made that offer yesterday when we were checking the other cabins. I guess he must have been in deputy mode and hadn't thought about the tree until later.

"Is he coming back for the rest of the logs?" There was still a sizable stack of them by the cabin. It had been a big tree, so I assumed they hadn't all fit in his truck. I wanted to offer him dinner if he came back, but neither mom nor I had been to the grocery store yet, so dinner tonight would probably be the same as it was last night—the luncheon meat and chips we'd brought with us. Logs aside, I felt like I should at least cook the guy a decent meal in repayment for his help.

"He said he was going to leave you some to use as seats around the fire pit, or even burn ourselves, as well as some of the kindling. Seems Friday-night bonfires are a big thing at the campground, and he noticed our wood pile wasn't very big." Mom spun around in the desk chair and handed me a stack of papers. "I printed off what the campground has done for the last four summers in terms of events as well as the coordination with the town and lake festivals. I know you'll want to put your own spin on things, but I figured that returning guests might have certain expectations and it would be a good idea to have some consistency with previous years to smooth the transition."

I took the papers, then leaned down to kiss her cheek. "Mom, you're a genius. Thank you."

These would be a huge help in planning, and it would allow me to get the jump start on that proposal I needed to turn in to The Bird by Friday. I was pretty sure Len's previous campground activities had passed her muster, and would be a good foundation on which to build what I wanted to do for the year.

"I posted up a calendar with each month—April through October." She pointed to the papers she'd tacked to the wall. "And put a hard copy of the reservations in a binder. I'll update it daily, just in case the power goes out or the computer catches fire or something. I like to have a paper backup, you know. I'm old-fashioned that way."

I was as well. I looked over at the calendars, each one color coded with percentage occupancy for both the cabins, the RV pads, and the tent sites. It would be a lot for Mom to maintain, but it made for a nice visual and a quick reference without having to login to the reservations system.

"I'll make sure this all gets transferred over to the office." I grimaced, remembering I hadn't even been in the office yet. There was supposedly a second computer there. I hoped it was functional.

Mom waved a hand at me. "For now I'll just work here in the house. Eventually I'll want to be at the office regular hours, though, so campers can pop in to buy supplies and bait."

I remembered all the ideas I'd had about selling fresh baked goods, toiletry packets, and local items when we'd first put in our offer on the campground. I really should head into town tomorrow and check out some of the stores to see if they'd consider selling their goods on consignment in our camp store/office. Just talking to mom about all this brought that wave of excitement back. I was a whole lot less anxious than I'd been earlier. Yes, this was a huge undertaking, the sort of risk I'd never taken in my life before. But Mom and I could make this work.

And wasn't taking a risk the whole reason I'd bought this place? I'd always played it safe, but facing my own mortality had put things in a new perspective for me. I'd wanted to do something fun, something different. I'd wanted to run my own business, have the freedom to really let my creativity fly.

And never wear a suit again—the very suit I now had on.

Heading back to my bedroom, I changed my clothes, then grabbed my cleaning supplies from this morning, taking Elvis with me on a long leash. We did a quick circuit of the campground, then headed over to the laundry. I was tickled pink to see nice stacks of clean, carefully folded sheets and towels, ready to go. Even the fitted sheets were in tidy squares, unlike the balled-up mess that resulted when I tried to fold them. Mom had really been busy today. I hoped she hadn't overdone it exertion-wise. She was probably thinking the same about me. I was still trying to get my strength and endurance back. But I'd spent three hours sitting in planning meetings to balance out the morning cleaning, so my exhaustion was more mental and emotional than physical.

I looked at my cleaning bucket, trying to be realistic about what else I might be able to accomplish today without having to spend tomorrow on the couch or in bed. Five cabins were clean and just needed linen on the day of the guests' arrival. We had reservations for five on Thursday, so honestly the other cabins could wait. But I really should have an additional five ready for impromptu guests. If our early season was going to kick off with a bang, I wanted to be prepared.

Two more. I'd clean two more cabins today, then call it done. Tomorrow I'd check all the RV sites, and maybe see if I could get the mower started. But for tonight, I'd go over the campground activities records and start thinking about what I wanted to do for this year. And I'd do it all after dinner, while relaxing on the couch with my feet up and a nice cup of hot tea.

But before I got to cleaning, I wanted to check out the state of the office.

I walked Elvis over and tied his long leash to a sturdy porch post. The tiny building that housed the office and the camp store was behind the owner's house and closer to the lake. The wooden steps creaked as I climbed to the porch, but they seemed sturdy. I made a quick note to look into the cost of adding a handicapped ramp, then unlocked the door.

A musty smell hit my nose, telling me that no one had probably opened this door in six months. There was definitely a computer behind the desk, but it was so old that it had slots in the front of the CPU for floppy disks. Hopefully it wasn't so old that it wouldn't run the reservations system, but I wasn't counting on it. There was a good chance that Len had just used the computer inside the house for the last decade or so of his life, and this thing was a giant paperweight.

I couldn't help myself. Instead of locking back up and returning to cleaning the cabins, I started here in the office. While the ancient computer was booting up, I pulled everything off the shelves and gave it all a good wipe down. Paper towels and toilet paper went back on the shelves. I threw the mini toiletries into a box, planning on making little convenience packs instead of selling everything individually. The office had a bathroom, so I spent most of my time making it sparkle, then cleaned up the rest of the building. By the time I was done, it smelled fresh and lemony. *I* smelled far worse, my ultra short hair plastered to my scalp, and my shirt splotchy with sweat.

I stood back and admired my work. The wood shelves and floor gleamed. The coffee station in the back sparkled, ready for our first guests. Taking out my phone, I made a quick list of what I wanted to stock in the store, and what businesses in town I'd need to pitch my proposal for consignment sales to.

With a quick check on Elvis, who was napping on the office porch, I went over to the computer. It was still making whirring and clicking noises I hadn't heard since my son was in diapers, but it *did* work. It had some sort of internet box attached to a connector on the back, but it didn't want to connect to the WiFi from the house, so I made another note to pick up a signal extender, or possibly even a hotspot device. I'd love to be able to supply internet to guests within a range of this office, putting some tables and chairs both on the porch and out front for guests to sit and hopefully immortalize their amazing vacation experience on social media.

The computer had a basic database for camp store sales, and a detailed inventory of supplies down to the pen. Once more, I admired Len Trout's incredible attention to detail. What his sons had supplied us during our due diligence had been thorough. Len Trout may have had a soft spot for gambling, boozing, down-on-their-luck maintenance men, but his records had been pristine.

Using the screechingly loud dot-matrix printer, I printed out a history of camp store sales, but the ink ran out after the third page. I made another note to buy more printer ink. Actually to buy another printer, since I doubted I could even find ink cartridges for this one unless I had a time-machine.

Packing up my cleaning supplies, I left, locking the door behind me. Elvis peered up at me with his sleepy hound-eyes, stretching and yawning as I untied the long leash.

"I feel ya, boy," I told the hound, stretching as well.

We staggered back to the house. I was satisfied with the day's progress, but I knew I had a whole lot more to do this week—including a whole lot to still do tonight.

Elvis, on the other hand, had nothing on his agenda but dinner and another nap.

CHAPTER 8

"Where the holy heck are the movers?" I fretted, knowing full well that Mom didn't have the answer to that question, but needing to vent. It was nine o'clock at night and no one had shown up today. It was dark, and we'd given up that we'd have our household goods before bedtime at this point.

Another night on the sofa. I scowled just thinking about it.

Mom held up her hands. "They haven't called me back. Did they say they'd definitely be here today?"

I blew out a breath, running my hands over my crusty, sweat-dried hair. "It was sort of a 'we plan to be there' thing."

It had been decades since the last time I'd moved, and that whole thing had been a blur. I'd been numb from my husband's affair, numb over his leaving, numb over not being able to afford the mortgage on my salary alone, even with the child support payments I hadn't wanted to completely rely upon. His mover had shown up on time to collect the items he'd received in our divorce settlement. Mine had shown up an hour later and hauled what remained to a storage facility ten miles away while Colton and I moved in with my parents. There I'd licked my wounds, eventually buying a reasonably priced townhouse for my son and me once Richard's and my home had sold.

My whole world had crashed to the ground then. And twenty years later, my world had crashed to the ground again. I'd reacted very differently both times. My divorce had sent me into survival mode, carefully saving every penny, trusting no one—not even myself. The cancer had broken the safe/stability part of me, turning the ant from the Aesop's fable into the grasshopper. The difference was that when I was dealing with cancer, I'd been responsible to no one but myself. Colton had grown and gone, was successful and married, and living in Dallas. Mom had been living with me for almost ten years, but although her savings were modest she had enough money to live on her own if I'd lost this battle.

It had just been me. And "me" had suddenly realized that life was painfully short. I'd beat cancer. And I wasn't about to waste any of the precious time I'd been gifted with in playing it safe.

"I'll call the movers again in the morning," I told Mom. "And go into town to talk to various businesses about supplying items for the camp store. I cleaned the office up, and although we need a new computer and printer, it's not bad."

Mom frowned. "Sassafrass Louise Letouroux. You have done too much today. I worried about this, you know. The world is not going to end if you don't get every single thing done in this campground by midnight tonight. Or by Thursday."

I sighed. "I know, Mom. Five cabins are ready to go, and

the office is ready. I just have a few more things I need to get done this week. Then I'll relax."

Relax. Corporate Me scoffed. *As if.*

I did feel better than I had this morning, though. I felt prepared. I actually felt energized about the progress I'd made. But at the end of the day, there was only so much cleaning and planning I could do. If I didn't have a handyman or someone to repair those two cabins and do other maintenance work around the campground, I'd be building a business on shaky ground. I didn't want our guests to come in three days and see two cabins in such a state of disrepair. I wanted them to see a well-run, well-maintained campground. The well-run we were on track to achieve. The well-maintained we still needed to handle.

"I put a notice on the Reckless Neighbors app this morning for a new handyman," I confessed to Mom. "It feels disrespectful to be doing that not a day after we found our current one dead in one of the cabins, but I won't rest easy until those two cabins are fixed and we've got someone who can do mowing, driveway leveling, and repairs."

I also wouldn't rest easy until Daryl Butts's murderer was apprehended. I didn't want to voice that out loud, to worry Mom, but the memories of that body in cabin three had haunted me all night and through the day.

And last night. I thought about the dim, reflected light, about Elvis's howl. It had probably just been an animal, but after having our handyman turn up dead in one of our cabins, every little thing seemed tinged with menace and danger.

"You sit," Mom scolded, giving me a hard look. "You look like you're ready to drop. I'll get dinner ready."

She'd had a busy day as well, but I complied knowing that it wouldn't take much effort to throw together sandwiches using the luncheon meat we'd brought with us, get out that half-empty bag of chips, and grab us a couple of soft drinks.

Collapsing onto the squeaky sofa, I put my feet up on the battered coffee table and settled in to look at the printout from the office computer. On Friday, Saturday, and Sunday the campground had traditionally hosted bonfires at the huge firepit by the lake. Len had sold s'mores kits and collapsible forks to roast the marshmallows, hotdogs, or whatever else the campers wanted. I made a note in my planner to continue that tradition, including putting up some Bluetooth speakers and playing music for some background ambiance. Once a month I'd try to get a local band in, scheduling them for the busiest booking days. The campground beer and wine retail license had transferred in the sale, and I hoped to expand the selection to include local products, craft beers, ciders, and maybe even meads and seltzers.

Mom plopped a plate with a ham and swiss on sourdough in front of me, Dijon mustard oozing out of the crust here and there. I smiled in thanks, took a bite, then read on, brainstorming ideas of my own. Kite festival. Fire-pit cooking contest. Shamrock festival. Drumstick Dash 5k. Pirate Day. Walleye fry. Fishing contest. Chili cooking contest. Disco mountain bike race. Art show and sale. Reckless triathlon. Innertube regatta. Lake ghost tour. Fireworks. Apple harvest festival. Monsters on the Lake.

I grinned, totally in my happy place as I wrote down plans for both regular weekly events as well as monthly ones. Then I looked over the summer festivals The Bird had discussed in today's meeting and shuffled things around on a tentative schedule.

I'd just finished my sandwich and was about to set the papers aside when I heard a knock on the door. Elvis leapt off the couch, instantly awake. I had a momentary spike of fear, but his wagging tail and happy grin made me realize that whoever was at the door was a friend, not a foe. At least by Elvis's standards, and I trusted my bloodhound.

I waved for Mom to stay seated and got up, stretching my stiff legs a bit as I made my way to the door. I opened it to find Jake Bailey with a young man next to him.

The boy looked to be in his late teens. He was on the short side, but had broad shoulders and a strong, stocky build. Curly brown hair flopped over a tanned forehead, and dark eyes stared at me with barely repressed excitement.

Jake put a hand on the boy's shoulder. "This is Austin Schaffley. He's graduating high school in a few months and is looking for a summer job."

"I get out of school at two," the boy chimed in. "I can work afternoons and evenings and on weekends, then come in earlier in the summer."

I glanced back and forth between Austin and Jake, settling on Austin. "What sort of work can you do?"

He grinned, shifting his weight from foot to foot. "I can clean cabins and mow. I can paint boats, the docks, and signs. I can hang up lights, start the bonfires and get chairs set up. I got a little bit of carpentry experience, so if you need a board replaced or something, I can do that."

No roof work, but I'd kind of reconciled myself that cabin six's repairs would need to be done by a professional.

"Think you could tackle the wobbly railing on cabin three's porch?" I asked. "Replace the rotted porch floorboards, and the warped boards on the docks?"

He nodded vigorously, then flipped his hair out of his eyes with one hand. "Yes, ma'am."

"Austin's dad works for Meadowland Homes over in Derwood," Jake explained. "They're one of the builders in the area doing new home construction."

"I had a summer job with them last year," Austin added.

"But I'd rather work for you here in the campground. If you'll have me, that is."

I was always a sucker for polite, enterprising, young boys and girls. It was one of the reasons I'd bought so much popcorn, wrapping paper, and cookies over the years from scouts, band kids, and Little League players.

I threw out the hourly rate that Len had been paying Daryl Butts, figuring that Austin would make up for his lack of experience in eagerness and hustle. The boy nodded at the sum, and I sent a grateful smile Jake's way before turning back to the boy.

"When can you start?" I asked.

"Tomorrow?" he asked hopefully.

"Deal." I stuck out my hand and he nearly ripped my arm from the socket with his enthusiastic shake.

Austin jogged back to Jake's truck, but the other man lingered. I stepped onto the porch and closed the door behind me.

"Thank you for cutting down that tree," I told him.

He nodded. "And thank you for the wood."

"I owe you more than wood for that," I told him.

He waved the offer away. "We're practically neighbors. Someday I'll need a favor, and we'll call it even."

I had no idea what sort of favor Jake Bailey would need from me, but if he wasn't going to ask for payment, then I wasn't going to press him on it.

"There's another reason I came over tonight," he continued. "I wanted to update you on last night."

My good mood evaporated. "Did you find out what happened to Daryl Butts? Who…who killed him?"

Jake shook his head. "Stef ruled cause of death as blunt force trauma to the head. She said it looked like there'd been a bit of a struggle beforehand—some scratches and abrasions consistent with fighting, but not enough time for bruises to form."

I sucked in a breath. "It couldn't have been too big of a fight. Nothing in the cabin was broken or knocked over or anything. Unless the killer straightened up the room before leaving."

Jake shot me a strange look and I did a mental head-slap. Right. Because someone who gets into a fist fight with another man, then bashes him over the head with something, would take the time to tidy up afterward, leaving a body and pool of blood behind.

"We're done with cabin three, by the way. I took the crime scene tape down just now, so you're free to go inside and do whatever you need to do."

I thought of asking Austin to clean it as well as fix the porch, then grimaced. Having a teen clean up dried blood where a man had been found dead? Uh, no. I'd clean it myself, and Austin could get started on the porch and pothole repairs when he got off school tomorrow.

I thought once more about last night, and debated for all of two seconds whether or not to bring it up. Taking the plunge, I went ahead and let Jake know about the dim light, Elvis's reaction, and the unlocked door. By the time I was done, I felt like a total idiot for being worried. It all sounded so silly.

"It was probably a bear. Or a raccoon," I finished. "I know they can open trash cans, so maybe they can open doors as well. Although there wasn't anything in the cabin food-wise, and I was sure we locked the door that night when we were searching the cabins."

Jake looked over toward the line of cabins, his expression inscrutable. The silence stretched on. Just when I was about to speak up, Jake did.

"I don't think what happened to Daryl Butts is related to

the campground," he said. "Daryl was a gambler and a drinker and got into his share of scuffles at the Twelve Gauge. I'm sure it was just a fluke that he met his end here and not on some dead-end dirt road, but I don't want to discount what you saw."

I blew out a breath, relieved that he didn't think I was a city-girl nutcase, freaking out over the local wildlife.

"It probably was an animal," he went on. "And I'd suggest you have Austin look at that lock, because it might not be latching properly. But just in case this sort of thing happens again..." He pulled out a pad of sticky notes, writing his name and phone number on one and handing it to me. "I only live across the street up the mountain. Oliver is handling the investigation about Daryl's death, but if you see anything suspicious—even if you think it's a bear or a raccoon—call me and I'll come down to look."

Oliver. The sheriff. I glanced at the sticky note, thinking that I should probably figure out the sheriff's last name eventually.

"You said Daryl hung out at the Twelve Gauge?" I asked, not remembering any business in town by that name.

"It's a lake-front bar outside the town limits." He scowled. "It's not the sort of bar you'd want to visit. It's rowdy. Only serves beer and shots. Got some illegal gambling in the back room that everyone turns a blind eye to."

"A dive bar!" My excitement rivaled Austin's at that moment. I adored seedy bars. Although if Daryl Butts had been getting into fights there, maybe this was a different sort of place than the colorful local hangouts back home.

Jake's expression turned pained. "I don't recommend you go there, ma'am."

"Sassy." I stuck the sticky note in my pocket. "Call me Sassy. And thank you again for cutting down that tree. And bringing Austin by for a job."

"You're welcome." He dipped his head and turned to leave. Just as he'd gotten to the porch step, I remembered something I'd forgotten to ask Lottie about earlier.

"Hey, Jake?" I waited for him to turn around. "I saw that people signing up to be on a pickleball team get three alewives. What the heck is an alewife?"

CHAPTER 9

Reckless Neighbors app:

Would the person throwing losing lottery tickets in my yard please stop. It's littering. And I don't need a daily reminder of how much money you're spending on scratch-offs.

Community yard sale on Dorsey Street, Saturday from nine to four. Kid's clothes, toys, housewares, craft supplies and more. Early birds will be shot. Show up before nine and leave in a casket.

Stumpy's Antiques and Oddies wants your old stuff! Clean out your attic, bring it in, and maybe walk away with some $$$.

I was awake early again the next morning, popping a few aspirin and hoping the movers showed up today with my mattress. Elvis had woken me again in the middle of the night, growling and staring intently out the window. I grabbed a flashlight before taking the hound out to check. No sooner had we stepped off the porch than I saw a fat furry animal shambling across the grass. Elvis let out a howl and the animal paused, turning his masked face to look at us, illuminated by the glow of the flashlight.

It had been a raccoon, and I'd had quite a few stern words

for Elvis as we walked back inside about how this couldn't continue to be a nightly thing.

Exhausted as I was from cleaning yesterday and a second restless night in a row, two cups of coffee and a brisk walk with Elvis had me feeling less achy if still a bit tired.

Alewives. My face burned hot with embarrassment. It had been bad enough telling Jake about some wild animal messing around in one of the cabins and my being afraid it was the murderer come back to kill us all. But then to find out that alewives were a type of bait fish. They were some sort of herring primarily used to catch lobster and crab, but in places like Savage Lake they were used to catch bass.

I knew nothing about fishing. Guess I was in for a learning experience owning a campground on a lake where fishing was king. When I'd come to stay here as a kid and as a parent, I'd been more interested in the hiking and canoeing than fishing, but this was clearly a sport I'd need to get educated on—especially if we were going to provide bait, fishing poles, and other supplies in our office/store.

Glancing at my to-do list, I prioritized, taking my need for a less strenuous day into consideration. I still had all day Wednesday to get ready for our guests and get the other cabins cleaned, but I really wanted to at least get to cabin three this morning. The idea that Austin, or an impromptu camping guest, could accidentally walk in and see the bloodstains worried me. I was sure that Jake had locked up after he'd taken the crime scene tape down, but I'd definitely breathe a sigh of relief once that cabin was cleaned.

The *rest* of the day I hoped to schedule less physical tasks.

The note in the Reckless Neighbors app about the Easter Bunny making the rounds on the local fire truck had given me some ideas for our kick-off week. There'd be the usual bonfire on Friday night, as well as the egg decorating and campground egg hunt I'd been thinking of. In addition to that, I wanted to host a Peep show.

No, not *that* kind of peep show!

Every Easter our town had hosted a community art exhibit that featured dioramas made entirely of Peeps—those sugar-crystal-coated marshmallow chicks that were almost a seasonal gag gift. Both children and adults had joined in the fun, and some of the artwork had been actually pretty impressive.

I was thinking it would be fun to do something similar, only with a time and supply limit on the crafts. At the bonfire Friday night, each guest would get three boxes of Peeps, toothpicks, and cardboard, and be responsible for assembling the iconic marshmallow figures into a work of art.

We'd display the finished sculptures as the night went on, and we'd sell vote tickets at ten for a dollar. The winner of the Peep diorama would win the cash. Or, I could even host it as a fifty-fifty award with the remaining funds going to the local food bank.

I needed to drive into the larger town of Derwood anyway for things like a new printer, an internet hotspot, and some things I wasn't sure I could get at the little stores in Reckless. While there, I'd stock up on Peeps plus get groceries so Mom and I had more to eat than just sandwiches and chips. Then on the way back to the campground, I'd swing by some of the local places in Reckless to see about consignment items for our camp store.

So much for my relaxing afternoon. I'd only had two cups of coffee and I already had the day packed with plans and activities. Shopping was high on my list, but it would have to wait until tomorrow if the movers were coming early today. There was no way I wanted Mom to have to deal with all that solo, so my plans for the day would need to be flexible.

A man picked up on the fifth ring at the moving

company. I introduced myself, then politely inquired about when I could expect the delivery of my household goods, trying to not let my irritation at the delay in delivery convey across the line.

"Of course, Ms. Letouroux," he replied with a cheerfulness that was at absolute odds with my own mood. "Let me just look here and see where the truck is. Ah yes. Wichita."

"*Wichita?*" My blood pressure went into the danger zone. "We're in Virginia. The truck left Maryland two days ago. Why the...why is it in Wichita?"

I'd almost said a curse word. That's how upset I was. But profanity wasn't going to get my household goods here any faster. In fact, it might actually cause the movers to delay them further. So I took a deep breath and tried to calm down.

"Well, the house we loaded after you was headed to Wichita, so we needed to go there first. Can't unload your stuff until we unload theirs," the man informed me.

It made sense, but no one had told me that when I'd booked this moving company. In fact, I was pretty sure they'd told me the delivery would be the next day. I was suspecting that they got this Wichita client at the last moment, and conveniently neglected to inform me about the change in plans.

"So when should I expect the delivery?" I was actually proud of how calm and not-annoyed I sounded.

"Once they unload in Wichita, they'll be coming your way," the man informed me. "So possibly tomorrow or the next day."

I held the phone away from my face and did a silent scream. Tomorrow. Or the next day. I'd possibly be sleeping on the couch for another two days, drinking instant coffee for another two days. I'd have to do laundry because I didn't bring a week's worth of clothing with me when I put a duffle bag of clothing into the SUV.

But there was nothing I could do or say that would make the truck drive faster. I thanked the man, asking him to please call me and keep me informed about the progress of my delivery, then hung up.

Guess I was going in to Derwood today after all. And while I was there, I might as well pick up another air mattress—one that didn't leak. And a coffee pot.

Or we could use the coffee maker in the office. It was sized to brew what looked to be three gallons of coffee at a time, but I might be able to reduce that and make enough for Mom and me. We both drank a lot of coffee, and we needed to start working in the office anyway. Plus we were getting guests in another two days. We'd want to have coffee ready for them as well.

Guests in two days. With my luck, the movers would arrive just when our guests did, completely screwing up the serene campground ambiance I'd wanted to project.

But there was nothing I could do about that. If a huge tractor-trailer pulled in to unload right when guests were arriving, I'd just have to deal with it—and hope they could unload quickly and get going.

Grabbing a granola bar and the remains of the chip bag, I ate as I restocked my cleaning bucket. Then I patted a snoozing Elvis on the head, and headed to cabin three, hoping to burn off my frustration and anger with some good old-fashioned cleaning.

The door was locked. As I fumbled with my key ring, I sent a silent "thank you" to Jake for ensuring the place was secure. Opening the door, I sucked in a breath and rescinded the "thank you."

The place was a wreck. White powdery stuff was all over

the floor and the furniture. The blood pool had dried into the hardwood with a solidity that made me wonder if even bleach could get the stains out. I sighed and started right where I stood, making several trips to the camp bathhouse to dump out and refill my mopping bucket. What I'd hoped would be a half-hour job took two hours. By the time I took the bedding off and tossed it on the porch to take to the laundry, I was ready for a nap. It was a good thing I now had Austin to help out, because there was no way I could manage all of this on my own.

And the floor… I'd cleaned up the blood and mopped, but the oak was more like untreated wood than the sealed and oiled floors I'd had back home. Hauling the buckets and cleaning supplies back to the owner's cabin, I added a few things to my grocery list. There was an old trick I'd learned to get spilled red wine and blood stains out of wooden cutting boards, and I was hoping it would work on the floor. Otherwise my only options would be to stain or paint the floor, or buy a rug.

Mom was up when I came in, working away on the computer with one hand while she drank coffee with the other hand. She looked up at me, and her smile faded.

"Sassy, you need to take it easy today. Let that young man you hired do the cleaning and repairs. You didn't buy this place to run yourself into the ground. You're supposed to do the planning and events. I'm supposed to do the reservations and run the campground store."

"Daryl Butts was supposed to do the maintenance, grounds keeping, and mowing." I ran a hand through my short hair. "But he obviously can't, and I didn't want Austin cleaning up that blood and all that stuff they sprinkled all over the cabin to look for fingerprints. Do you know how hard that stuff is to get up? It gets all thick and goopy with water. I must have gone through eight buckets of wash water, and I still think there's a film on the floor. Plus I can't get that bloodstain out of the wood."

"Baking soda and vinegar," Mom suggested.

"I know," I snapped, then took a breath to calm down. I was tired and cranky, but that was no reason to bite Mom's head off.

"No more cleaning today," Mom scolded, taking her hand off the keyboard to wave a finger at me. "Go buy groceries then visit that Coffee Dog place and relax there to do your planning."

She was right. I'd only been here two days, but I needed to get away. Otherwise I'd just sit here and fret over the cabin six roof, the bloodstain in cabin three, all the work that needed to be done so we could give a good impression to our guests.

"I'm calling roofers today to get estimates, so you just take that off your list right now." Mom glared at me, as if I was going to argue. "I'm also going to order the toiletry items we need for the camper kits, as well as beach towels for rentals. And when the movers show up, I'll handle that as well. The only thing that needs to be on your mind today is buying groceries and thinking up all the fun things we're going to do here at Reckless Campers Campground this season."

"The movers aren't showing up today," I said, reminded by her statement that I hadn't told her of my early morning conversation. "The truck is in Wichita with all of our stuff in it. We'll be lucky if they're here tomorrow, but it's probably going to be Thursday."

Mom's eyebrows shot practically to her hairline. "*Wichita?*"

"Don't ask," I grumbled. "I'll pick up another air mattress today when I'm shopping, because another night on that couch is going to put me in the hospital."

I honestly wanted to burn the darned thing once we were

settled in with our own furniture. Although setting a ratty floral-print couch from the seventies on the Friday night campground bonfire might not be in keeping with the image I was trying to project.

Taking Elvis for another quick walk, I headed for a shower. Buying groceries and supplies didn't warrant getting cleaned up, but I intended on stopping by some of the stores in Reckless to see if they'd offer their products on consignment in our camp store, and I didn't want to go in looking like I'd just cleaned a crime scene.

CHAPTER 10

*D*ressed in my last clean pair of jeans and a T-shirt, I grabbed my keys and hesitated as I saw Elvis standing by the door, staring at me with his mournful gaze, his tail slowly wagging.

"I can't take you, buddy." I reached down to scratch behind the hound's ears. "You'd just be sitting in the SUV while I shop, and that's no fun. I promise we'll go on a longer walk tonight. And this weekend, maybe even a hike."

I'd be busy this weekend, but I'd try to make time for my dog. He'd been so patient with all this moving and the chaos of the last few days. I knew he was getting bored being cooped up in the house so much. Once campers started arriving, he'd have more opportunity for fun. Kids to play with. Maybe other dogs to play with. Splashing in the lake and greeting people as they came to the office/camp store. I'd just need to make sure I kept an eye on him so he didn't steal anyone's food. It would be bad for business if my hound made a habit of scarfing down everyone's dinners.

With a whole lot of guilt, I patted the dog once more and headed to town. My shopping excursion in Derwood resulted in a whole lot more purchases than I'd originally intended. Mom had said she'd order the items for the camper packs and some towels, but given my recent experience with the movers, I was concerned the shipments wouldn't arrive in time for Thursday's guests, so I grabbed enough supplies and towels to get us through the week in addition to an air mattress, some Bluetooth speakers, a printer, and an extender for our Wi-Fi. Cringing a bit at the total, I ran my debit card through the machine. I'd budgeted for some start-up expenses, but this plus the repairs were going to push that budget to the limit.

With everything in the trunk of my SUV, I swung by the grocery store, loading items needing refrigeration in the two coolers I'd brought with me. It was March, and I was pretty sure the milk and meats would be fine in the car for a few hours, but just in case I'd packed the coolers with the old ice from the campground machine before I'd left, adding the need to schedule ice deliveries on the endless to-do list.

Tired and ready for a break, I drove back to Reckless, pulled into the municipal parking lot and headed for The Coffee Dog.

The aroma that filled my nose as I walked through the door made me realize just how horrible the instant coffee I'd been drinking for the last two days had been. A teenage girl stood behind the counter. Her curly hair was pulled back, but a fringe softened the edge of her hairline. She smiled, and dimples creased her golden-brown cheeks.

"Welcome to The Coffee Dog. What can I get you?"

I went to order a coffee, and my stomach growled, reminding me that I hadn't eaten since my meager breakfast.

The girl's dimples deepened. "We're known for our Reubens."

"Sold," I told her. "A Reuben and a latte."

She nodded in approval. "Skim, whole, almond, or oat milk in your latte?"

"Whole please." Life was too short for skim milk.

"For here, or carry out?" she asked.

I thought of Mom's lecture about relaxing a bit. "Here, please."

She rang the order up and I paid, lingering by the register as she called the food order to the back and made my drink.

"Is the owner or the manager in?" I asked as she handed the drink over. "I'm the new owner at the campground and I wanted to talk to someone about supplying coffee as well as some bagged breakfast and lunch items."

"Oh, how cool," she exclaimed. "I'm glad someone bought that place. We were all worried it would end up being condos or something. Mom is in the back. I'll ask her if she's got a second to talk."

I sat at a table, glancing around at the handful of other people eating their lunch and looking at their phones or reading a book. Taking a sip of my drink, I sighed. Now *this* was the way coffee was supposed to taste. Dark. Rich. A luxurious nutty roasted flavor with just the right amount of bitterness. And the milk balanced it all out, making me feel like I was having a decadent treat.

The woman that brought my sandwich out was the spitting image of her daughter only with her hair in long twists and covered with a bright pink bandana.

"I'm Sierra Sanchez-Blue," she introduced herself, sliding me a business card as she set the plate in front of me.

A business card. That was one more thing I needed to get done. Mom and I needed business cards and flyers. I eyed the embossed logo of a basset hound with a monocle sipping a cup of coffee, and wondered who'd designed their adorable logo.

"I'm Sassafrass Letouroux." I motioned for her to sit across from me. "Call me Sassy."

"Please call me Sierra." She smiled as she sat, the same deep dimples in her cheeks as her daughter. "Flora said you bought the campground?"

I nodded. "My mom and I are going to run it. I'm hoping to buy bulk coffee from you for our coffee maker as well as food. Plus small bags of coffee I'm hoping to sell on consignment in our camp store."

"Absolutely." Sierra pulled a notepad and a pen out of her apron pocket. "Len used to order his coffee online, even though I tried to get him to use us instead. I'm thrilled at the chance to get your business."

I took another sip of my coffee, thinking that I was the one thrilled here. There had been an industrial-sized can of Folgers Original in the back room that I'd tossed, worried that being open for the last six months would make the stuff undrinkable. I had nothing against Folgers, but I really wanted the campground to be a part of the town. If we highlighted the businesses here in Reckless, became a part of the community, then they'd have an interest in helping us succeed.

And if the last two days were any indication, we were going to need as much help as we could get.

"I'm not sure how much coffee we'll go through to begin with," I warned her. "We've got a handful of cabins booked for Thursday, as well as a few RV sites. I don't know how many people are coming though or if they're coffee drinkers or not."

"Pffft." Sierra waved a hand. "Everyone's a coffee drinker. Let's see...I'd estimate two per cabin. The RVs are most likely families, so count them as two adult coffee drinkers and two kids each. Although a lot of the RV folks tend to pack their own stuff, they might be interested in picking up a small bag of something roasted and made locally to try out."

"You roast your own beans?" I asked, a bit surprised.

She nodded. "I didn't start out roasting, and I'll admit that some of my blends include beans I've bought pre-roasted, but I have a few that are one-hundred-percent mine."

I glanced at the back of the small shop, and she laughed.

"The roasters are at home. I converted one of our garages, much to my husband's chagrin."

"Where do you find the time?" I wondered, thinking that this woman's to-do list definitely rivaled mine.

She waved a hand. "I run and mind the roasters at night when the shop is closed. And the kids help as well. Plus, I like keeping busy."

Me too.

I did the math, trying to estimate how much coffee we should get to start out. "How about I get three pounds for this week, then I'll increase it once the season kicks in and we have more guests."

Sierra wrote it on her pad. "We'll grind it fresh for you each week. Just keep it sealed up tight. If it looks like you're running out, give me a call and I'll send Flora over with another bag."

"Thanks." I frowned in thought. "Maybe quarter-pound and half-pound bags for sale in the store?"

She nodded. "I'll send a couple of different roast types, and you can let me know what's selling best. Why don't you take five bags with you today just so you have some inventory? Or I can have Flora deliver it all on Thursday, so it's fresh ground. I'm assuming you'll want her to come out each day with the food order?"

I mulled over that. "How about if I ask guests to preorder their breakfasts and lunches? I don't want food going to waste." Or me spending money on food that was going to waste.

Sierra pursed her lips, then waved the pen at me. "How about we do some snack-packs. They'll have nuts, dried fruit, a granola bar, and some humus and crackers. They'll keep in the fridge. That way you'll have something handy to sell if someone didn't order a go-lunch and wants to go on a day hike."

"That's a great idea," I told her, excited that I'd stopped in here. Sierra was clearly a savvy business woman, and I was thrilled to be partnering with her.

She made another note. "I'll put together a menu of lunches and breakfasts that you can post in your camp store. Just call or text me the orders each night and I'll have Flora drop them by in the morning."

This was amazing. "Thanks. I really appreciate this."

She stood, a smile once more creasing her cheeks. "Thank *you* for the opportunity. I'll have Flora get your order together while you eat. How about you pay upfront for that three pounds you're taking home today, then the rest is net thirty? Due on the first of the month? I'll have Flora check the consignment inventory once a week and swap out anything that's not selling, then I'll invoice you end of the month."

"Perfect." I watched her head back to the kitchen, so relieved that I'd be working with someone so organized and enthusiastic. Then I took a bite of my sandwich and realized that Sierra Sanchez-Blue's organizational skills weren't the only incredible thing about The Coffee Dog. The Rueben was amazing. This was definitely a sandwich I hoped made it to the campground menu.

I finished my lunch, doing absolutely nothing except enjoying the food and relaxing. No checking e-mails. No fussing over the campground. No feeling frustrated about our movers. Nothing but a great latte and a truly outstanding Rueben. When only crumbs were left on the plate, I drank the last drop of my latte, bought my three pounds of dark roast from Flora, and headed out.

I was feeling the effects of the prior day's activity, but pushed on, stopping by the Bait and Beer after my lunch break. The business was in a squat cinder block building with soda vending machines flanking the entrance. A set of garage bays off to the left had me wondering if the place had once been a repair shop. Or maybe it still was.

Walking in, I didn't see any vehicles being repaired, or even a spare spot for an automotive shop. The left and back walls were lined with refrigeration units holding an endless selection of beer in cases and six packs. The units also had plastic pint and quart containers that I assumed contained bait. I wasn't sure how the health department would feel about the bargain lager being kept in the fridge next to containers of nightcrawlers. Maybe they didn't care. It wasn't like the worms were going to escape from the plastic containers and somehow manage to get inside sealed cans and bottles of beer.

Two men were sitting on folding lawn chairs playing Parcheesi on top of a barrel. Two other men stood nearby, chatting and drinking beer. A dark gray pig sat beside them, apparently watching the game with rapt attention.

Squeakers. No doubt if I checked the Reckless Neighbors app, I'd find that Celeste Crenshaw was once more posting about her missing pig. The animal was larger than I'd imagined. Not quite as huge as the market pigs I'd seen at the fair growing up, but not quite a pet-sized mini pig either. Squeakers was about the height of a German Shepherd, and probably weighed over two hundred pounds. He oinked at the Parcheesi game in progress, and one of the players turned to the pig.

"Don't need you micromanaging my game, you porcine oaf. You wanna comment, then you can play the next round."

"He ain't got opposable thumbs," the man's opponent commented.

"He ain't got fingers at all," an onlooker chimed in. "But he still can scoot the pieces around the board. He beat you last week, Truman. Might not want to push it too far with the pig."

Truman glared, apparently not cowed at the idea of insulting the pig. I rang a little bell at the counter since no one seemed to have noticed there was a customer in the store. The men and the pig ignored the bell, but a short, thin woman with bright gold hair came out of the back room. She shot the men and pig a look that should have withered them on the spot, then turned a smile my way.

"Can I help you?" she asked.

For the second time today I was regretting my lack of business cards.

"I'm Sassafrass Letouroux. Sassy. I own the campground and I wanted to talk about selling a selection of bait in our camp store on consignment."

She shrugged. "Sure. I'll offer you the same deal I did Len. I'll drop bait off once a week. You're responsible for keeping it refrigerated. You get twenty percent of sales. I'll keep an accounting and you pay me each Monday for what sold. Sound good?"

I'd hoped for a thirty-day billing period like Sierra had offered, but I wasn't really in a position to bargain. I might be able to buy coffee online, but I knew nothing about bait. I had no idea what people needed to use to catch fish in the lake, or how long it kept. Did bait spoil? Even refrigerated bait?

"Sounds good," I told her, reaching out to shake her hand.

"I'm Bobbi Benjamin, by the way." She glanced over at the

men and the pig. "And that's the four Stooges. Five, if I include Squeakers, which I do."

"Are they here every day?" I asked.

She rolled her eyes. "Every. Single. Day. It's Tuesday, so it's Parcheesi on the barrel today. Tomorrow they'll be playing Trouble. Friday is Monopoly, just in case you're interested."

"No women," the man who'd called Squeakers a porcine oaf said. "Only men and pigs allowed."

"Because I'd whoop your butts at Monopoly, that's why," Bobbi replied before turning back to me. "When do you want the bait, hon?"

"Thursday morning?" I had no idea if the guests coming in for this weekend planned to fish or just hike, but it would be best if I were prepared.

"Got it," Bobbi announced. "You need anything else? Beer?" She eyed Squeakers, biting back a smile. "Bacon?"

The pig squealed, and Bobbi laughed. "Just kidding, bud. I don't know about the rest of this town, but we don't eat the customers here."

"I'm good for now, thanks." As tempting as it was to grab a six pack of beer, I was a bit of a lightweight as far as alcohol went and was far too busy to spend the rest of the day and evening snoozing on the couch.

"Then I'll see you Thursday," Bobbi told me.

I waved at her, then cast a quick glance at the men and the pig, all of them deep in thought over the Parcheesi game, as I left.

On the way back to my car, I saw a sign and made a quick detour. I was exhausted, but while I was in town and nearby, I figured I might as well check out that antique shop Lottie had told me about. It would be great if I could unload some of those books and make a few quick bucks. Even if it was just enough to pay for the coffee I'd just purchased, I'd be happy.

Stumpy's Antiques and Oddities was in a rowhouse wedged between a locksmith and a store selling semi-precious gems and local artwork. I went in, smiling at the familiar smell of dust, damp, and camphor that always seemed to permeate any place dealing in old furniture. Stumpy's was a mix of estate sale and garage sale with some decent silver-plate in a glass display case right alongside bundled packs of stainless-steel teaspoons marked ten for a dollar. A bald, rotund man with a set of jowls that reminded me of my bloodhound stood behind the counter, berating a younger man who had thin dark hair in a low ponytail, and a sullen set to his jaw that belied the downcast gaze.

The older man broke off his tirade at my entrance and forced a smile to his face. "Can I help you?"

"I hope so. Lottie Sinclair told me you might be interested in buying some old books? I'm Sassy Letouroux. My mother and I bought the campground. There was some stuff left behind, including hundreds of old books."

I could swear the man's ears perked up at the words "old books."

"Stumpy Miller." The man extended a hand across the counter. "What sort of old books are we talking about here? Classics? Good stuff, or dime store romances?"

I bristled a little because I'd spent a good portion of my life reading romances and put them firmly in the "good stuff" category. But I didn't want to get into an argument with a man who might be willing to pay me cash to haul away a bunch of books I didn't want—mostly because they *weren't* dime store romances.

"I haven't done an inventory or anything, but the ones I looked at seemed to be non-fiction," I told him. "One about bird migration, and the others on history. They're all hardback except for a few paperbacks here and there. No romance. No mystery."

Which sucked. If there had been some romance books or even mysteries, I would have been tempted to toss my ever-growing to-do list and chill by the lake with a book in my hands and Elvis by my side.

Stumpy wrinkled his nose then turned to the younger man. "Lucky! Run over to Miss Letter-o's place and take a look at those books."

I opened my mouth to correct him, then shut it, figuring it wasn't worth the bother.

"Len Trout didn't throw nothing away," Stumpy continued, his attention back on me. "Books are heavy. I'm betting his sons weren't interested in packing all that up and hauling it somewhere. I'm betting as well that they didn't bother because none of those books were worth anything. But I'll send Lucky over for a look-see. If some are in good shape, they might be worth taking to the flea markets."

Drat. I'd hoped to unload the whole lot, but it was looking like I'd be wasting a day of my time supervising Lucky only to have him leave with five books and me with a handful of change. I briefly thought of throwing them on the Friday-night bonfire, but that would give even more of a bad impression than my setting fire to an old couch. I didn't want to be known as that woman who burned books. Plus I was seriously worried about the bad karma involved in tossing books into the flames. They might be boring, but I still counted books as almost sentient beings, and burning them edged close to murder in my mind.

"I'm going to be kind of busy for the next few days," I said to Lucky, who had his back to me as he fiddled with some frames in a box. "When do you think you'll be able to come by?"

"Tomorrow morning?" he asked, his back still to me. "You

don't have to be there if you've got things to do. Just show me where the books are and I'll sort through them real-quick. If there's some hardback ones in decent shape, I'll make you an offer. Those sell good at the flea markets."

I felt a little uneasy about having a man I didn't know in my house alone, but it wasn't like there was anything for him to steal. I doubted Lucky wanted that ratty floral couch, or the duct-taped chairs at the table.

Lucky. Hadn't Jake mentioned something about a Lucky Miller getting his hand stuck in a soda machine trying to steal a Mountain Dew? I doubted there were two men in Reckless named Lucky, and if Stumpy's last name was Miller, this was probably his son or nephew or something.

Now I was less worried about Lucky stealing something from the house and more worried about him losing a hand in the garbage disposal or getting stuck trying to climb up the chimney. Lucky seemed like a rather ironic name for this man.

"Tomorrow morning sounds good," I told him, even though I really didn't have the time. It would be good to get at least some of these books gone before the movers arrived. And maybe I'd get lucky and Lucky would take a liking to the floral couch as well.

I wrote down my name and number on the back of one of the shop business cards they had by the register and slid it over. Lucky didn't take it, probably because he still had his back to me and couldn't see it, but Stumpy picked up the card.

"Can you call me when you're on your way?" I asked. "I should be around all morning, but I might be cleaning one of the cabins or working in the office. Let me know when you're coming and I'll meet you at the house. That's where the books are."

Duh. Like they'd be anywhere else. I mean, there were a

few books in each of the cabins—three, to be precise—but I didn't want Lucky taking those. Actually I should probably restock the cabin that only had two books before he came. I doubted the man was going to want to buy everything filling the shelves on either side of the fireplace, but it might be nice to pick out books that had something to do with fishing or the history of the area to put in the cabins.

He turned to give me a quick glance, then went back to the frames. "Sure."

At least I didn't have to worry about the guy talking my ear off as he went through the books. Judging from his demeanor, he'd probably take a quick glance over the shelf, grab one or two, and be out of there in all of five minutes.

This part of my trip had been a total bust.

Getting rid of the books wasn't really at the top of my priorities list. It wasn't like I'd even need the shelf space after the movers arrived. Neither mom nor I were big on knick-knacks. Still, I had books of my own I wanted to put on those shelves. If Lucky didn't want them, and I managed to get everything ready for our first group of guests, maybe I'd take some time and box them all up. I could ask Austin to move them to the garage and I'd figure out what to do with them later. If I was lucky, maybe some elves would come in the night and take them away. If I was unlucky, then I'd have to find a place that would want the books. Or resign myself to whatever bad karma would come from hauling them all to the dump.

CHAPTER 11

*A*ustin was already at the campground when I pulled down the long drive. He'd somehow managed to find the riding mower and was halfway through mowing the areas where the tent campers set up. It already looked better having the weeds knocked down. He waved at me and I waved back, sending a silent "thank you" to Jake for bringing the boy over.

I quickly unloaded the groceries, putting the perishables in the fridge, emptying the ice from the coolers, then setting them out back to dry. Neither mom nor Elvis were in the house, so I drove the SUV around to the office, thinking I'd find them there.

My hound was tied to the porch post, snoozing in the early spring sun. He yawned when he saw me, getting up and giving himself a good shake before greeting me with a wagging tail.

"We'll have a long walk tonight," I promised him, ruffling his floppy ears and planting a kiss on his forehead before heading inside.

Mom was working on the ancient computer. She'd taken

the travel-sized toiletries I'd pulled off the shelf and assembled them into kits, putting each set into ziplock bags. Little price tags were tied to each with brightly colored curly ribbon.

"This is cute," I exclaimed, picking up one of the kits.

"There was a box of wrapping paper and ribbon in my bedroom closet." She laughed. "If only I could have found a coffee machine in my closet. Or a set of pots and pans."

I pulled the three pounds of coffee out of my shopping bag and set it on the counter. "I've got the coffee problem solved. We'll just use the big machine here in the office until the movers get here. There are packets of filters in the storeroom. This should last us the week, unless we suddenly get a ton of unexpected guests."

I told Mom about my successful day shopping and my trip to The Coffee Dog and the bait store. While I unloaded the SUV and set up the new printer, Mom got me caught up on her end of the business. She'd been busy not just putting together the little convenience packets, but in making calls. Two different roofing companies would be out Thursday and Friday to give us estimates on the cabin six repair as well as the porch roof on cabin three. Mom had stressed to both contractors that we needed the work done within the next week. She'd also ordered bulk supplies for the camp store, arranged for regular ice deliveries and for the beer and wine distributor to swing by in the next day or two.

Austin had arrived early, fixed the wobbly railing on cabin three's porch, then let Mom know what lumber to order for both porch and dock repairs. After that, he'd turned his attention to getting the mower up and running.

I blew out a breath, thinking through my timeline as I sorted through the printer cables. Cabin six would be unrentable for another week or two, meaning early guests would just have to see the unsightly blue tarp currently keeping rain and debris from the inside of the cabin. Frowning, I added another week to that estimate, thinking that even after the roof was fixed, the cabin probably needed a deep cleaning and possibly some inside repairs. The fate of cabin three was more optimistic. If Austin could get the porch floorboards replaced by the weekend, I could potentially rent it even with a small leak in the porch roof.

Of course, that was only if I could manage to get the bloodstain out of the floor.

It would all be fine, I reassured myself. Even with two cabins on the injured reserve list, we still had ten. If we had a surge of early seasonal guests, then I'd just have to offer a discount on a leaky-porch cabin three and put some pressure on the roofers to hurry on cabin six.

We still had the RV spots and tent camping areas, but this early in the season, most of our income would hinge on the cabins being rented. A few diehard folks might be willing to pitch a tent with the evening temps occasionally dipping into the forties, but that side of the campground wouldn't really get going until next month.

Once the printer was up and running, I got to work on the internet hotspot while Mom unboxed my other purchases and started filling the shelves. By the time we were done, the place looked like a real camp store with the toiletry kits, cans of sunscreen and bug spray, lighters, Firestarter, and tealight candles all neatly arranged.

Hauling in the cases of water, Gatorade, and sodas, I cleaned then stocked the fridge, breaking down all the boxes, and hauling them to the dumpster behind the office. Then I brought in the last of my purchases—the eggs, candy, art supplies, and Peeps. At the grocery store I'd realized that I didn't have the means or the time to be boiling dozens of eggs. I opted instead for non-edible plaster ones to decorate, and plastic ones to stuff with candy and hide for the egg hunt.

Putting the activity items in the storeroom, I stepped back into the store area and smiled. Everything was coming together. By the time guests arrived, we'd have bait in the fridge, snack-packs for sale, and an order form for boxed lunches and breakfasts.

"I'm going to make our first pot of coffee," Mom announced. "You go back to the house and take a nap, and I'll bring you a cup."

A nap sounded so good right now, but I knew I'd never be able to sleep with everything I still needed to get done.

"I'm going to try to get that bloodstain off the floor in cabin three," I told Mom. "I'll swing by and grab a cup of coffee when I'm done. Then I promised Elvis a long walk."

Mom shook her head. "Nap. That bloodstain isn't going anywhere, and that cabin isn't even rented for weeks. As for Elvis, he can have a long walk tomorrow. You need to rest."

"A short walk for Elvis," I countered. "I'll do one quick round with the baking soda paste on that bloodstain, *then* I'll nap. Or maybe relax on the sofa and read a book."

Mom sighed, clearly realizing this was a battle she wasn't going to win. "Okay, but I want you to take it easy tonight. Me too. Everything's ready for our guests. There's no sense in killing ourselves over stuff that can wait a few days."

She was right, but getting cabin three cleaned wasn't something that could wait. I had a feeling we were going to be full up come next week and I didn't want to turn a guest away because I'd needed an afternoon nap.

Elvis jumped up as I exited the office, his whole body wagging once he realized I was making good on my promise of a walk. Figuring I'd kill two birds with one stroll, I led the bloodhound around the campground, briefly checking the various outbuildings I hadn't had time to visit. The storage building, garage, and activities center looked to be in decent shape, although they could all use a coat of paint. The canoes seemed okay, but I wouldn't know if they were lake-worthy and watertight until we tested them. These were all jobs I planned on giving to Austin. Elvis and I wandered around the three amenities centers, and I made a mental note to also have Austin check the washers and driers as well as the ice and vending machines in the ones I hadn't used for cleaning the linens. The RV lots didn't look like they'd require much upkeep, but I hesitated at the dump station, wrinkling my nose.

I'd never camped in an RV or camper before, so I had no idea how these things worked in terms of dumping the gray and black waste water. Was there something I needed to do to ensure sewage didn't flood the campground the first time someone emptied their tanks? Were they hooked up to the campground septic, or on a different system?

I'd been so excited to buy this campground, but not for the first time, the overwhelming nature of the business washed over me. Would there ever be time for relaxing on the dock in the sun with a book? Long hikes with Elvis? Canoeing out on the lake on a Sunday afternoon? Or would I spend every waking minute racing around dealing with broken washing machines and flooded septic systems?

Type A, Corporate Me, loved the challenge, the chance to turn this place around. But the other me was already thinking of a vacation—a vacation that might never come now that I was a business owner.

Shaking off my gloomy mood, Elvis and I looped around the cabins. As we got close to cabin five, the bloodhound shoved his nose to the ground and began to cast back and forth.

"Got a scent boy?" I asked him.

Elvis had been bred and trained to track deer in his

youth, leading hunters to a downed buck that had run off after being shot. As much as I appreciated that Elvis's work had meant that deer meat hadn't gone to waste, I'd never been a hunter. Instead, I'd taken some search and rescue classes with Elvis back when I'd first adopted him, and found that in addition to the usual bloodhound independence and focus, he was particularly good at tracking a variety of scents.

There hadn't been much use for search and rescue where we'd lived, but maybe that was something Elvis and I could do here. For fun. In all that copious free time I was going to have with a campground to fix up and run.

Or maybe not.

Elvis yanked to the right, nearly pulling my arm from the socket. He strained at the leash, nose to the ground. I humored him, jogging along and keeping the leash in a tight grip, in case he tried to take off after whatever interesting scent had his attention.

We went from cabin five to the woods via a circuitous route that led behind a few bushes and several trees. The bloodhound surged down a trail, and I followed, protesting that this was farther than I'd intended. By the time I'd gotten the hound under control, we were in the woods, about a hundred yards from the campground.

Elvis finally sat as I'd been telling him to do with increasing volume for the last few minutes, while I looked around and caught my breath. It was a pretty trail, wide and well maintained. A sign a few feet up pointed to the left where there was supposedly an overlook, then to the right, announcing that the White Dove Trail parking area was only half a mile ahead.

"We'll check out the overlook later," I told Elvis, feeling guilty that "later" might be several days or even a few weeks.

The hound didn't know that, and wagged his tail at my

pronouncement. Dust stirred at the motion, the sunlight reflecting something shiny and silver.

"What's that?" I asked. "Move your big ole butt so I can see what's on the ground there."

Elvis stood, and I bent down to pick up what I figured was a candy wrapper or a piece of foil.

It was neither. My dog had been sitting on a key that had a bent and broken circular ring still looped through one of the grooves. I picked it up and turned it over, and found a colored strip of tape attached to the top of the key. On it, in faded black, was a number five.

CHAPTER 12

*W*e finished our walk via cabin five. Feeling a little foolish, I looped Elvis's leash around my arm, stepped onto the porch, and tried the key in the lock.

It fit.

I turned it.

The door opened, and a shiver ran down my back.

This was ridiculous. People misplaced keys all the time. It wasn't out of the question that some guest last summer had lost the key on the trail, and I'd just happened to find it. Or maybe it had dropped off of my huge ring of keys, and a squirrel or something had carried it up the trail before dropping it? There had to be a perfectly good explanation for why a key to the cabin was lying on the path of a trail.

But even with all those valid reasons running through my head, I couldn't help but notice the odd coincidence that this key fit this particular cabin—the very cabin I'd found unlocked two nights ago—the cabin with an intruder who might or might not have been an animal.

"It's okay," I said to Elvis as I locked the cabin once more. The dog looked up at me, not the slightest bit disturbed about this whole thing. "There are probably hundreds of duplicates of these keys," I told the hound as well as myself. "I doubt Len Trout changed the locks in decades. There are probably hundreds of copies of these floating around."

As we made our way to the house, I realized there might be hundreds of copies of those keys floating around as well. Maybe I should at least change the locks on the house and start budgeting to do the same on all the buildings over the next month or two.

In the house, Elvis sniffed at his empty food bowl while I gathered my cleaning supplies. Curious, I went over to the key ring hanging by the door and looked for the one to cabin five. It was there, right where it had been the day before, the yellow tape marked with a number five.

So the key I'd found hadn't been mine. It still could have been one lost long ago. I wasn't going to be a fool, freaking out over the coincidence of the cabin number. Because that's what it was—a coincidence.

I didn't want to leave Elvis in the house all by himself, especially with an empty food bowl, so I took him with me to cabin three, tying his long leash on the porch post then testing the newly repaired porch rail. Austin had done a great job, and the railing didn't budge with my pushing and tugging. He'd put a chalk x on the floorboards that needed replacing as well. Glancing across the newly cut grass, I saw him still on the mower, finishing up in the section devoted to RVs and trailers.

Unlocking the cabin door, I hauled my supplies inside and got to work on the stained section of the floor. First I sprinkled baking soda over the area, then used a brush dipped in white vinegar to gently scrub it into the unfinished hardwood. I said a quick prayer, then went over it with a damp cloth, cleaning up the paste and evaluating the situation.

It was better, but there was still a clear stain on the floor. I stood and eyed it, not sure if I should resort to bleach at this point or not. At least it didn't look like blood anymore. If I didn't know better, I would have thought the stain had been the result of a long-ago roof leak, or a spilled glass of wine.

Neither of those two were situations I wanted my guests thinking about while staying here. Bleach would most likely take the stain out, but it would also leave this section of the floor a noticeably different color than the rest. Refinishing the entire floor wasn't in my budget or my timeline, so I got back on my hands and knees and tried the baking soda and vinegar trick once more.

I was just getting ready to wipe up the second round of paste when I heard the door squeak open. Looking over my shoulder, I saw Austin.

"I'm done mowing and was going to get some of that stone from the pile behind the garage to fill in the potholes in the driveway." His gaze traveled to the mess on the floor and his expression sobered. "Is that where...Daryl died?" he asked softly.

I hadn't wanted him to see this. I hadn't wanted anyone to see this. Heck, I hadn't wanted to see it myself. Cleaning this up, it was all I could do to keep my mind from wandering back to that day and seeing the body.

"Yes. This is where Daryl died." I wiped away the paste, then stood and looked at the floor.

"It doesn't look so bad," Austin lied.

I knelt back down and wiped a rag over the floor. "If it still shows after the wood dries, I'm going to just to give up and put a carpet over it," I told him.

I hadn't thought of buying a throw rug when I was shopping today. Maybe there was an old one in the house somewhere I could use. Heck, if Mom found wrapping paper in her bedroom closet, there had to be a smallish rug somewhere—maybe in the attic.

"That might work," Austin replied, but his voice sounded distracted.

After a few seconds, I looked over to see him staring at the spot on the floor.

"Did you know him?" I asked softly. "Daryl?"

"Not really. I mean, I knew who he was and some of my family knew him. Reckless is a small town. We all kind of know each other." He took a deep breath, then blew it out. "It's just weird having his job. Makes me feel like I'm robbing the dead or something."

It wasn't his fault. The boy hadn't killed Daryl. But I understood his unease over the situation.

"I felt weird replacing him not a day after he died," I confessed to Austin. "But there's things I can't do here at the campground, and we've got guests arriving in two days. It might seem disrespectful, but I needed someone right away to do the job. And I'm really grateful you were available and could start today."

He nodded. "He wasn't as bad as people thought. Daryl, I mean. I overheard Dad say Daryl had a problem with getting in over his head in card games. Owed a lot of people money. And he drank, but honestly I don't think he was much worse about that than some of the other people in town. I know there were times when he didn't show up here on time or show up at all, but he wasn't mean. He'd never hurt anyone. And he was kinda honest in his own way. He didn't deserve to be killed."

I walked over and put my hand on the boy's shoulder. "No, he didn't deserve to be killed."

I'd been focusing so much on getting the campground up and running that I hadn't given Daryl's death much of a thought beyond the inconvenience of losing my handyman. Shame washed through me at the realization. A man had died. He hadn't been a perfect man—far from perfect it sounded. But he hadn't been someone whose untimely death should be shrugged off either. Was it the gambling debts that had led to Daryl's murder? It had to be the gambling because I couldn't imagine someone being killed over showing up late to work. And something like cheating at cards or a drunken argument would most likely have led to violence at the game or bar, not here in a little campground cabin. It had to be the gambling debts. Either that or Daryl had just been in the wrong place at the wrong time.

Once more I thought of the light, of Elvis howling at the cabin on the other side of the campground, at the shadow I could have sworn I saw. Bear? Or a person. Had Daryl interrupted an intruder who'd hit and killed him? Had that intruder not gotten what they'd come for and returned two nights ago? Was Elvis's presence the only thing that saved me from a similar fate?

I shook my head, feeling like a fool for letting my mind go down that rabbit hole. This was ridiculous. If Daryl had interrupted a robbery, then the criminal would have had plenty of time after killing him to steal whatever he wanted. There had been no one here at the campground. No one would have stopped him. Why flee, then come back the next night, when someone, namely my mother and me, were here and any robbery would be more complicated. Plus what on earth would there be to steal here? Len Trout's sons had taken everything of value, only leaving behind a bunch of rickety furniture, and evidently a box of wrapping paper in a bedroom closet. That theory just didn't make sense.

It had to be the gambling debts. Daryl owed someone big-time, and that person realized they were never going to get paid. They followed Daryl here and killed him while the man was making his rounds, secure in the fact that no one would notice in an unoccupied campground.

But there was that key…

"Do you know if Daryl had a set of keys to all the buildings?" I asked Austin.

The boy shrugged. "Probably. I mean, he was the maintenance man, so he'd have to, wouldn't he? You don't have to give me my own set though. I just started here, and I understand if you'd rather just have me ask you if I need to get into one of the cabins or other buildings."

I blinked, because my train of thought hadn't even gone there. Of course Austin would need a set of keys. It would be a huge waste of time for him to have to track down Mom or me every time he needed to clean a cabin or check the garage for something. Most of the other buildings wouldn't be locked up until off-season, but he should have access to a master set.

"I'm a bit swamped right now, but I'll get you a set as soon as I can go into town and make duplicates," I told him. "Until then, you'll just have to come ask me or Mom."

He nodded. "Ms. Letouroux Senior let me in to get the mower today. I don't mind waiting."

Where was the set of keys Daryl had? I wondered, barely registering Austin's comment. They were probably at the morgue along with all his other personal effects. It wasn't like I'd searched the man, or looked him over close enough to notice if he had a bunch of keys in his pocket or hanging off his belt loop. I'd need to ask Jake about them the next time I saw him. Hopefully there was some process where they could be returned to me, saving me a trip into Derwood and a long wait at the home improvement store key counter.

I was sure the morgue had them. Surely the murderer wouldn't have bothered to take them. What would a killer need with a set of keys to the campground cabins and outbuildings? There was nothing here of value to steal—at least that I'd come across.

"Go ahead and fill in those potholes. If you get those done, I wouldn't mind if you'd start cleaning the shower buildings, including the restroom areas. If you run out of time you can do that tomorrow though, as well as checking to see if the appliances work in the amenities buildings." I frowned, remembering the dump station. "And you wouldn't know anything about septic systems, would you? Specifically the one the RV and camper guests use to dump their waste?"

His eyes widened. "I've got no idea how any of that works, ma'am."

It was just as well. I got the idea that septic stuff was something I should probably call in a professional for. I gave Austin's shoulder a quick pat. "And if you get thirsty, stop by the office. My mother put on a pot of coffee, and we've got water, sports drinks, and sodas in the fridge."

"Thanks Ms. Letouroux," he said.

"Sassy," I told him. "Call me Sassy." Yes, I was probably old enough to be this kid's grandmother, but I'd never get used to being called Ms. Letouroux. That was Mom, not me.

He smiled. "Thanks Ms. Sassy. I'll let you know when I'm done for the day, just so you can keep track of my hours."

Good grief, I hadn't even thought of that. Hopefully Mom or Austin had noted down when he'd arrived, because keeping track of employee hours and running payroll was something I was absolutely not used to doing.

I watched Austin leave, hearing the smack of the screen door behind him. Then I turned back to the stain that was still clearly visible on the hardwood and sighed.

There were a *lot* of things I was not used to doing. Like cleaning blood off hardwood floors.

CHAPTER 13

*E*lvis and I headed to the office, where I poured fresh coffee into an ancient chipped mug that Mom had found in the storeroom, then returned to the house. After tossing and turning on the couch for half an hour in a fruitless attempt to nap, I finally got up, blew up my air mattress for later tonight, then surveyed our options for dinner.

No pots and pans. No microwave. I'd brought home a roasted chicken from the deli section of the grocery store, and was thinking I might be able to heat it up in the oven on some foil. That plus the pre-made potato salad and the loaf of French bread might have to do. If I ever moved again, I was packing at least a fry pan and a saucepan in the car with me. And my coffee maker.

"I almost forgot to show you this." Mom walked into the house, waving a stack of papers.

I looked up from the makeshift aluminum foil pan I was trying to craft. "What is it? More reservations for this weekend?"

Part of me hoped it was. The income would be a good thing. Part of me worried that we weren't ready for ten cabin rentals and a dozen RV sites. Had I bought enough Peeps? Should I ask Sierra at The Coffee Dog to send over another three-pound bag of dark roast?

"No, there are no additional reservations. But you'll hopefully find this just as funny as I did. That Len Trout was one organized man." Mom plopped the papers on the kitchen counter beside me. "Do you know he catalogued every single book in this place? The ones on the shelves, as well as ones stored in boxes in the attic? He's even got the ones in the cabins inventoried down to which three books are in which cabin."

I laughed, picking up the first two pages and looking over the list. "Good grief. How did he deal with the ones the campers took home with them? Cabin one only has two books on the nightstands. I'm guessing a guest in the fall must have decided they were up for grabs."

Mom shrugged. "I didn't go over the list in any detail. I swear there must be a thousand books in the inventory though. From what I've seen, he probably did mark the ones that got stolen from the cabins. He had some system of letters and numbers, and I didn't dig too far into figuring it out. I was more concerned with the reservations and printing off the prior schedule of events than a bunch of old books."

"Thousands?" I thought Mom might be exaggerating, but looking through the stack of papers, it did seem to be a whole lot more than what was in the cabins and on the shelves on either side of the fireplace.

Mom shrugged. "Maybe there are boxes of them in the garage or the boathouse? And he does have some marked as in the attic."

I looked upward at the ceiling. "Maybe he rented a storage unit somewhere and his kids left that for us to deal with as well?"

If so, I wasn't paying for it. Buying the campground didn't obligate me to pay for some offsite storage unit filled with boxes of books. Or wrapping paper.

This oddly detailed inventory made me feel even more reluctant to just toss the books away or burn them. Len must have read every one of these books if he'd cared enough to catalogue them. I envisioned an elderly man, sitting by the fireplace, deep into a tome on hummingbird migration, and chuckled at the image. The sentimental side of me now wanted to keep all of these books as some sort of tribute to the quirks of the previous owner. The practical side of me was fretting over where the heck I'd store them all. Even if a handful were taken from the cabins each year, it would take decades to even make a dent in this inventory.

"I wonder if there's enough room in the attic to store the ones down here as well," I mused. Space wasn't just a consideration, though. How much weight could the attic hold? There were a lot of books on these shelves, and who knew what else was up there.

"I've been thinking we should probably look up in the attic anyway," Mom said, her gaze also turning toward the ceiling. "If they left books and wrapping paper behind, there's probably a bunch of stuff up there as well."

I wasn't all that eager to find more junk I'd need to sort through, but the thought of attic storage gave me an idea. What if there were pots and pans up there? Dishes? More mugs? Silverware? A coffee maker? A throw rug that I could toss over the blood-stained floor in cabin three. With the way my luck was going, it was probably *all* wrapping paper and books, but it was worth a look.

"Let me put this chicken in the oven, and I'll go take a look." It might be better to look before I put the chicken in the oven. If I could find a cookie sheet or a roasting pan, it might mean the difference between a tasty chicken dinner or one that ended up ripping through the foil and landing on the floor.

"Actually, I'll take a quick peek, *then* I'll get dinner ready," I amended.

I headed into the master bedroom closet where the attic access door was, hoping I'd find some treasure up there—or at least a roasting pan.

Unfolding the wooden ladder, I climbed up. The place was packed full of items with boxes stacked next to weird miscellanea like a silver Christmas tree, some plastic holiday lawn ornaments, and what looked like an old high chair. A few of the boxes had been knocked over, their contents spilled everywhere.

Once more I felt a surge of annoyance at Len Trout's sons who'd not bothered to haul any of this stuff away. I was also irritated at our real estate agent, who'd clearly done the absolute minimum to get her commission, and hadn't let us know we'd have to deal with junk removal upon arrival. If I ever moved again, I was making sure it was in the contract that all furniture and household goods needed to be gone before closing.

Although our agent and Len's sons' laziness might work in my favor this time.

"Please let there be cookware," I whispered in a chant. "Dishes. Utensils. Anything."

"Is there anything up there?" Mom called from the base of the attic steps.

"Oh, there's a whole lot up here," I called back. "I just don't know if any it is useful or not."

Annoyed as I was, there was no real urgency to go through this stuff. I'd planned on using the attic for my own storage, but if I shoved some of these boxes over to the one side, there should be room for mine and Mom's items. I'd wanted to schedule a bulk trash company to come out next week to take things like the horrible floral couch and the broken dining room chairs. If I was going to pay for someone to haul a truckload of junk, then I really should add some of this in with the rest. It would save me the cost of having the company to come back and haul it away later.

And then I had an idea.

I might be able to use some of this stuff for campground activities. Not the Christmas decorations—at least not now —but there could be craft supplies, games, and other items that would spur my imagination and provide some fun for our guests.

"Worst case scenario, I'll send each camper home with a free book," I muttered. "Or maybe a box of free books."

"What's that, Sassy?" Mom called up.

"Nothing. Just talking to myself." I heaved my butt over the ledge and onto the attic floor. That's when I realized that although the roof wasn't tall enough for me to walk upright, I might be able to manage a sort of stooped shuffle. It would be better than crawling around in the dust.

The first box I grabbed was full of seasonal-themed decorative flags. I remembered seeing holders on the porch supports of each cabin, and rooted through the box, pulling out a handful with colorful Easter eggs printed on them. Thinking that these would be super cute and absolutely in keeping with my Peep-and-egg-hunt theme for the next two weeks, I pushed that box over to the opening. I could absolutely use the flags. There looked like there were enough for not just the cabins, but to maybe decorate outside of the office, and maybe even give one to each of the campers in the RV spots.

The second box was full of old clothing. That I shoved to the side to deal with at some indeterminant time in the future. I'd probably end up sending the contents off somewhere as a donation once I had enough time to really go through everything up here.

I made my way across the attic, checking the boxes and not finding anything beyond the flags that would be immediately useful. There were a few sheets of plywood across the rafters near the attic entrance, but beyond that, there was no floor to walk on. I kept my feet on the rafters, stepping over the boxes and trying to avoid touching the insulation.

"What's up there?" Mom shouted through the opening.

"A lot of junk," I yelled back.

So far there hadn't been anything remotely resembling kitchen items. I pushed aside boxes of plastic, outdoor holiday decorations, another box of tree ornaments, and half a dozen boxes containing more clothing. Other boxes had craft-making supplies, and small painting kits. I set those aside, thoughts of possibly hosting craft and paint activities in my mind. We could charge a minimal fee, have it all set up by the docks on the picnic tables during sunset. We could even sell bottles of wine and make it into one of those paint-and-sip nights. Or craft-and-sip. I didn't think our license included serving alcohol, but I knew we were allowed to sell bottles of wine and beer, so it would need to be a buy-or-bring-your-own affair.

My mind was distracted with all the extra activities we could offer our guests as I made my way toward the far side of the attic. This was where the majority of the boxes were. Even though these were smaller than the others, they were definitely heavier. Maybe pots and pans? Dishes? They were certainly heavy enough to hold dishes.

I opened one and as I looked inside, I saw why they were so heavy.

Books. Good grief, Len did seem to have a thing for books. Not that I counted that to be a fault. I too liked books —just not the same sort of books that Len did, evidently. I glanced at a few of them, my hope for a good rom-com or British detective novel fading as I looked through the non-fiction titles.

Checking a few other boxes, I saw that they held the same, and decided to give up. If there were housewares somewhere in this attic, they were buried behind a gazillion boxes of books, clothes, and holiday decorations. I pushed the box of painting supplies across the attic to the stairs. Grimacing, I thought of how my back would feel trying to carry this and the box of flags down the folding stairs. Maybe I should wait for when Austin came to work tomorrow and ask him for help. Or Lucky when he came over to look at the books in the morning. Then I remembered how unhelpful Lucky had seemed at the antique shop and decided I should pin my hopes on Austin instead. He was my best chance of getting these boxes out of the attic without ending up in a bed with a heating pad and a bottle of painkillers.

At the last moment, I decided to go back to the other side of the attic and grab a box. It was a smaller one that was light enough for me to get down the stairs on my own. I'd seen some puzzles and other games in there that would be nice to set up on the table in the office for rainy day activities.

I made my way across the rafters, stooped over so I didn't hit my head. Picking up the box, I turned around and stepped on something that threw my balance off. I dropped the box, waving my arms wildly as I fell backwards. Trying to catch myself, I stepped to the side, and my foot broke through the drywall into the living room ceiling. I pitched over to the side, my other foot slipping off the rafter and punching through the drywall as well. The whole thing crumbled under my weight and I threw myself across one of the rafters, holding on for dear life.

CHAPTER 14

*G*ripping onto the rafter, I tried to shift my weight forward enough to pull my legs out of the ceiling and back into the attic. As I moved, more of the drywall broke apart and several of the boxes crashed through into the living room.

That's when I decided the best thing I could do was hold very, very still and hope that I didn't fall completely through and drop the ten feet onto the oak floor.

"Sassy!" Mom's shout from down below was clear as could be—probably because of the giant hole I'd just made in our ceiling.

"I'm okay," I called back. At least, I thought I was okay. I was breathing. Nothing felt broken. Although I was probably going to end up in bed with that heating pad and painkillers after all.

"What are you doing up there?" Mom shouted. "Your legs are sticking out of the ceiling."

Yeah. Great observation powers there, Mom.

"My foot slipped off the rafter," I replied. "The drywall couldn't hold my weight."

Another box fell through, landing below with a crash. I winced, hoping Mom was clear of the falling debris. This was just peachy. Now I'd need to find the money to repair the ceiling I'd just damaged in addition to the cabin roof.

Although the more immediate problem was that I was trapped here, with both legs poking through the ceiling. I was afraid to move and risk the whole thing collapsing down, but I was going to have to figure out how to get out of here without dying or breaking any bones. After all, I could hardly spend the rest of my natural life like this.

Adding to my woes, my shirt had hiked up when I'd fallen and that nice thick layer of insulation was up against my skin. I was already beginning to itch just thinking about it.

"Mom? Is there a tall step ladder in the garage?" If I could somehow get my feet on the ladder and get my weight on it, then maybe I could scoot upright, bust the rest of the way through the ceiling, and just walk down the ladder to safety. My ceiling was already ruined. Me breaking a larger, Sassy-sized, hole wasn't going to be any worse than the holes I and the boxes had already made.

"I'll check. Hold on," she called up.

"That's pretty much my only alternative," I mumbled, hoping she got back before my arms gave out and I fell.

Mom was gone for a while. My arms were starting to ache. And my nose itched. Why do noses always itch when you've got no way to scratch them? It was one of life's eternal mysteries.

I heard the door slam and had a moment of hope.

"There's no ladder in the shed," Mom said.

There went my moment of hope.

"So I called that nice sometimes-deputy, Jake. His name and number were on a piece of paper on the kitchen counter."

How mortifying. Although her calling 911 probably wouldn't have been any better. Shelly would have wasted an hour asking questions, then probably called Jake anyway. Mom doing so just saved us all a lot of time and aggravation.

Jake. I went to hit my forehead on the attic floor, then decided that might not be the best idea given my current position. The guy would think I was a total idiot. First I was freaking out over what was probably a raccoon or a bear in one of the cabins, and now I was dangling through my living room ceiling. This was not the impression I wanted to make on the locals.

I heard movement down below, then a sound as if something were being dragged across the floor.

"Mom? What are you doing?"

"Just making sure if you fall down you don't break something."

By break something I wondered if she meant a bone, or a lamp. At that moment, the drywall made an ominous noise.

"Mom, get out of the way," I warned.

There was a crack sound, and the box to my right fell through to the floor.

"Oh, my goodness! Hold on, Sassy. Don't move. I've got an idea," Mom called out.

I heard her footsteps heading in the direction of the bedrooms, then a more dragging noises. Another box shifted.

"Watch out, Mom," I shouted. "More stuff from the attic might be falling through the ceiling, and it's heavy."

I might be falling through the ceiling, and I was heavier than these boxes. Either one of us could kill my mother by landing on her.

"Hold on," Mom repeated, sounding somewhat closer.

I heard more dragging sounds.

"Mom, stay back!" I shouted.

Just then another box fell through the ceiling. Instead of hearing the crash of it hitting the floor, the only sound was a muffled thump and a gasp that I assumed came from my mother.

"Mom?" My voice squeaked in panic.

"Oh, I'm fine. It landed on the sofa cushions. My, what a lot of books there are in this box!"

"Sofa cushions?"

"And the air mattress from your room," she said. "I'm moving these books out of the way, then I'm going to go get another mattress and maybe some pillows. That way if you fall through before Jake gets here, you won't crack your noggin."

The air mattress. The brand new air mattress that I'd just bought. With the way my week was going, that box had probably poked a hole in the thing. I sighed, realizing that I might be spending yet another night on the couch. Maybe two.

The air mattress and sofa cushions *were* a good idea. I'd still be dropping down ten feet. It was better than nothing, but there weren't enough air mattresses and pillows in this house to truly cushion my fall.

This whole thing might be embarrassing, but Jake couldn't get here soon enough, in my opinion. Hopefully Mom told him to bring a ladder.

The thought had barely crossed my mind when I heard a knock at the door. Then I heard swearing. Mom never swore, and the voice was male, so that clued me in that my rescue had arrived. And not a moment too soon. My arms were killing me.

"Did you bring a ladder?" I called down.

"No. Hang on. Don't move."

I heard footsteps running, and the creak of someone

climbing the attic ladder. Then I saw Jake's head poke up through the attic entrance.

He swore again.

"You taking the Lord's name in vain is not helping me here," I shouted, worried that I wouldn't be able to hold on much longer.

"How the he…heck did you do this?" he demanded.

"Can we save the humiliating story for when I'm safely on the ground?" I really needed to do more exercises, maybe pick up some small dumbbells the next time I was at the big-box store in Derwood so I could work on my upper body strength. Although it wasn't like I planned on hanging for dear life, dangling through my living room ceiling ever again.

Jake wove his way around boxes, hopping from rafter to rafter like he was a professional tightrope walker. Finally he stood in front of me, surveying the situation.

"I'm going to grab you under your arms and pull you up," he informed me.

"You sure you don't have a ladder somewhere?" I asked, worried.

I had grave doubts about the success of his plan. First of all, although I wasn't a large woman, I wasn't exactly a light-weight either. Jake looked like a strong guy, but bending over and deadlifting me through the living room ceiling seemed a bit beyond his abilities.

"Maybe you should lie down across the rafters," I suggested. "That way if you drop me, only I'll go crashing to the floor."

"I'm not going to drop you." He widened his stance and reached down. "And I won't have enough leverage to lift you if I'm lying down. Ready?"

"No, I'm not," I said as he grabbed me under my arms.

"Well, too bad."

He pulled and lifted me about a foot up, then tightened his grip and pressed me against him. My face was about knee level, and I was hoping it wouldn't go higher. I desperately wanted to pull my legs up and try to ease myself back into the attic, but I was worried that me moving or shifting my weight would knock him off balance and send us both through the ceiling.

With a grunt, Jake stepped back with one foot onto the rafter behind him, then shifted his weight before following with the other foot. The movement slid me further up through the drywall, and far enough into the attic that I could raise my knees and pull my legs onto the solid wood supports.

"You good?" Jake asked before slowly lowering me back down.

I lay there, spread across the rafters, safe, and relatively unharmed. This could have turned out so much worse. I might have wound up dead or with a broken neck. What would Mom have done if I'd died or been seriously hurt? I needed to be more careful. I couldn't risk that something would happen to me leaving her solo at the age of eighty-five with a campground to manage on her own.

Jake helped me to my feet, holding onto my shoulders to steady me as I got my balance. I'd have plenty of time to wallow in embarrassment later. Right now all I felt was gratitude that he'd gotten here on time and gotten me out of a dangerous situation. I was definitely counting my blessings, and Jake Bailey was one of them.

"You good?" he asked again.

I smiled up at him. "I think so. Thank you. Honestly, thank you so much."

He shrugged, still holding onto my shoulders. "It was nothing. Glad I could help."

"Sassy! Look what I found!"

I looked down at Mom's voice and saw her through the

hole in the ceiling. She was holding something up—something rectangular and metal.

A roasting pan.

"Would you like to stay for dinner?" I asked as I turned back to Jake. "We're having chicken."

CHAPTER 15

*M*om and I both insisted Jake stay for dinner, pestering him until he gave in and accepted. We left the slowly deflating air mattress where it was, just in case more boxes fell through the ceiling. Jake brought in a tarp from his truck and went back up to the attic to place it across the opening as well as move boxes away from the damaged area.

While he was doing that, I cleaned up the mess in the living room as best as I could, then I showered, trying to get the insulation fibers off my skin. I looked a mess, a huge red rash across my stomach and rashes all along my arms. I had bruises on my legs and midsection. Most of my body probably would be a colorful black and blue by tomorrow.

By the time the chicken was warm and on the table, I was as clean as I was going to be. The hole in the ceiling was covered by a blue tarp, and Jake assured us that we wouldn't be woken in the middle of the night by the contents of the attic falling down on our heads.

Not that I'd probably get much sleep. As predicted, there was a hole in my brand new air mattress. Picking the sofa cushions off the floor, I shook them off outside, then put them back where they belonged, resigning myself to one, if not two, more nights tossing and turning on the old couch.

Jake, Mom, and I sat down with paper plates and plastic utensils to eat our roast chicken, potato salad, and bread. Sadly the box with the roasting pan did not include any other kitchenware aside from a pair of hot dog tongs.

"So what sort of work did you all do before buying this campground," Jake asked as he dug into his chicken.

"Marketing and corporate event planning," I told him. "I specialized in trade shows, but also organized the big annual sales trip, the smaller monthly meetings, and some executive meetings."

It had been fun, and I hoped that the enjoyable aspects of that job would transfer over to my new enterprise.

"I've been retired for a while, but when I worked, I was a secretary," Mom said. "Back in those days the job was called 'secretary' and not administrative assistant. I took notes in shorthand, transcribed dictation from these huge reel-to-reel recording machines, and typed everything on a manual typewriter. I was beyond excited when we upgraded to electric."

"I learned to type on a typewriter as well," Jake commented. "An IBM Selectric."

"That was some super high-tech stuff back in the early sixties," Mom said.

Jake laughed. "Well, they were pretty old in the late seventies when I was learning to type. I remember wishing we had the newer kind with the correction tape in them."

"Correction tape was a game-changer," I remembered. "No more shifting the page up to smear Liquid Paper on the mistake, blowing to make it dry faster, then desperately trying to line the page back up again. With the Liquid Paper, my corrected letters were always a hair higher or lower than the rest of the line."

"The real game-changer was computers," Mom chimed in.

"Mom's been taking courses at the local college for decades," I told Jake.

"I'd taken a few courses at a computer store in the late eighties and decided you're never too old to learn something new," she said. "By then Sassy and Quint were out of college and on their own. Owen and I were financially comfortable, so I quit my secretary job and became a professional student."

"What sort of classes did you take?" Jake asked.

Mom waved a hand. "Oh, anything that struck my fancy. Mostly software and computer stuff, just in case something happened and I needed to go back into the workforce again, but I also took classes in art history, photography, women's poetry…"

"Underwater basket weaving," I teased. "Mom, you should check out the college here and see if there are any classes you might want to take."

"I won't have time for that with this campground business," she said. "Besides in my free time, I've been writing a book."

"Really?" I smiled, loving the idea that there would be a memoir of Mom's life to pass down to future generations. "So, what do *you* do besides being a sometimes-deputy?" I asked, turning to face Jake.

"Right now?" he shrugged. "Work on my house. Repair fencing. Take care of the horses."

"You're a rancher?" I asked, assuming that from his comment about horses.

"Not in the commercial sense. I used to be a police officer —mounted park police, to be exact. I've always loved horses, so when I retired down here, I adopted a bunch of the equally-retired police mounts. We're a grumpy bunch, all hanging out up on the mountain, trying to keep the roof from falling in on our heads." He chuckled. "At least *I'm* trying to keep the roof from falling in on our heads. The horses are more concerned with the quality of their hay and if there's a new mineral lick in the run-in."

"You run a horse rescue!" I exclaimed, considering Jake with fresh eyes. I hadn't gotten the grumpy vibe from him at all—more like the stern, professional vibe. I'd been right about the police thing. He still made me want to jump to attention with a glance, worried about what I might have done wrong that deserved a ticket or even arrest. But I'd never once thought of him as running a horse rescue.

"It's not like I'm a non-profit or anything," he protested. "I just have eight horses that needed a soft place to land when their service was done. I felt it was the least I could do."

"Do you have any horses you were partnered with when you were an active duty officer?" Mom asked.

"One." Jake looked down at his plate and pushed the potato salad around with his fork a bit. "He partnered with another officer after I retired, but I kept an eye on him. Last year, when he had a suspensory injury, I offered to take him on. The vet costs just about bankrupted me, but he's sound now and enjoying life."

"What's his name?" I asked, because that was important.

"Keno Kicker." Jake smiled, the lines around his eyes softening as he talked about his horse. "Three-quarters Thoroughbred and a quarter Clydesdale. Tall, big-boned chestnut boy with a white star and two white socks. Kick's sorta like a racehorse who spent a lot of time at the gym doing presses and curls. Thick neck. Thick shoulders. More lean muscle in the back-end. Fast as heck. Well, he *was* fast as heck back in the day. Which is probably how he got himself injured."

"He sounds beautiful," I told Jake, blinking back some sudden tears. I cried about everything the last few years. I wasn't sure if it was menopause or what, but around the age of fifty-five, I'd become a sentimental old fool.

Who was I kidding? I'd always been a sentimental old fool.

And I'd always had a soft spot for people who rescued animals.

It took a special kind of person to take on the trauma, the health conditions, and often the genetic defects that came with a dog who'd been abused, hoarded, or just plain old dumped. Elvis had been named by the rescue I'd adopted him from, and it had fit my hound perfectly. He was so handsome, even right now when he was snoring over in the corner of the living room with drool dampening the hardwood floors. Black and tan, with droopy ears, droopy eyes, and jowls that went on for miles.

"Kick's twenty-five," Jake told me. "I'm not sure how much longer he or the other guys have, but I'll give them a good life until the end. And just between you and me, I've got my eye on another horse from New York who's probably heading for retirement in the next few months."

I didn't know why that needed to stay between us and him. Adopting another horse didn't feel like the sort of thing he'd need to keep a secret, but so be it.

"It's not hard to set up a non-profit organization," Mom said. "Or a quick website highlighting your horses and encouraging donations via PayPal or some other service. People love helping animals and rescue organizations, and the extra money might help pay for feed or hay or fence repairs."

Jake took a last bite of his potato salad, then pushed the plate away. "I'll think about that, Ms. Letouroux. Honestly, I like this being something just between me and the horses, but I'll think about it. Thank you for dinner, but I really need to get going here. I've got to check on the horses and bring them in for the night."

I stood as well. "Thank *you* for coming out to help me. I don't know what I would have done if you hadn't been available."

I would have eventually lost my grip and fallen, that's what would have happened. The air mattress might have cushioned my fall, but I'd have still risked serious injury.

"No problem at all, Miss Sassy," he replied, reminding me of Austin with his form of address. "Would you mind walking me outside a bit, so I can have a word with you?"

Mom's eyebrows shot up, but I didn't see anything untoward in Jake's request. I figured he probably wanted to update me about Daryl Butts's murder.

Five steps off the porch toward his truck, and he confirmed that was exactly what he wanted to discuss.

"I just wanted to reassure you that the sheriff has a strong suspect in conjunction with the murder of Daryl Butts," he told me as we walked. "He hasn't made any arrests yet, but I'm sure it won't be long now."

I let out a relieved breath. "Oh good. Was it the gambling thing? Someone he owed money to?"

Jake nodded. "Daryl did owe this man a substantial amount of money from a card game the month before. He wasn't getting paid, and witnesses had seen the two arguing several times. Four days ago, witnesses say the suspect threatened Daryl with bodily harm if he didn't get his money in the next twenty-four hours. I'm not privy to the other details of the case, but the sheriff feels confident that he's the murderer."

"That's great news." I'd rest a lot easier knowing that a murderer was behind bars awaiting trial—and that my campground had nothing to do with this murder other than unfortunately being the place where the killer caught up with his victim. "So I'm guessing he confessed? Your suspect?"

Jake snorted. "Hardly. They usually don't until there's a plea deal on the table though. He'll protest and claim he's innocent until his lawyer talks him into taking a deal."

"Still, it's good to know the killer will be off the streets," I said.

Jake nodded. "I also wanted to let you know that I did talk to the sheriff about your incident the other night. He said our suspect has a solid alibi for that night, so it wasn't him sneaking around your property. The sheriff also said that during the interview it was clear that the suspect didn't have any reason to return to the campground."

"So it must have been a raccoon after all. Or a bear." I stopped and turned to face Jake. "You must think I'm a total idiot. My mother tells me there's a dead body in a cabin, and instead of calling 911 right away, I go look for my wandering hound. I panic over wild animals nosing around an unlocked cabin. I fall through the attic half into my living room."

He smiled. "To tell you the truth, I would have looked for my dog first as well. The rest? Well, I'm not questioning your intelligence at all, I'm just thinking you might be a little bit in over your head here with this place."

That was a true statement—so true that it didn't even sting.

But the murderer was caught, and I didn't need to worry about any threat to the campground, my mother, my dog, or myself.

CHAPTER 16

*R*eckless Neighbor App:
Only two more spots left on our pickleball team! Sign up now at the Community Center, and get your three free alewives!

Goat for rent. Got brush? Weeds? Just hate mowing? Rent Dilbert for a week and he'll eat your yard clean. Call Eric for details and to schedule.

I woke up the next morning reasonably well-rested compared to the previous two nights. The couch was still insanely uncomfortable, but Elvis didn't wake me growling at whatever animal might have been roaming about the campground last night. He was either getting used to the critters that lived around here, or my furry intruder had decided to take the night off.

I took my hound for a walk, then headed over to the office to get a fresh pot of coffee brewing. While I was waiting, I went ahead and organized the craft materials for the weekend. I had the egg decorating supplies sorted, and twenty plastic eggs stuffed with individually wrapped

Tootsie Rolls and Hershey's Kisses when the coffee finished brewing.

It was amazing to walk back to the house with Elvis and a cup of real, honest-to-goodness coffee. There I got my hound some breakfast, grabbed an apple and a granola bar, and sat down to sort through my plans for the week.

Austin was handling the rest of the cleaning. All the deliveries were scheduled. Contractors would be over in the next two days to give us quotes on the cabin repairs. The activities I'd planned were almost ready. The camp store was stocked, and the consignment items would be arriving tomorrow. All I needed to do was finish that festival coordination plan for The Bird, pray the movers arrived, and let Lucky into the house so he could sort through and pick out whatever books the antique store wanted to buy.

Oh. I jotted a quick note to check the RV sites today. I wanted to make sure the water and electrical were working at each of the pads, and that the grills and picnic tables were clean and in good condition. Just as I wanted to make sure we had as many rentable cabins ready to go as possible, the same held true for the RV spots.

If there were any electrical or plumbing issues, I'd need to call in a licensed repair person since I doubted that was something Austin could do. Even if there were a few problems here and there, I was betting enough of the RV sites would have functioning water and electricity to serve the guests arriving tomorrow. I crossed my fingers, hoping I didn't need to deal with the high costs of an electrical or plumbing rush-job.

I could hear Mom stirring in the back bedroom, so I quickly grabbed Elvis for another run to the office. She was in the kitchen eating a cold Pop Tart by the time I returned with a mug of coffee for her.

"Bless you," she intoned as she took the outstretched mug. "So what's on our agenda today?"

"Some last-minute double-checking and organizing." I smiled. "I think we're good, actually. It's a bit of a relief to know we're ready for guests."

"I'll see if we have any new reservations." Mom grinned. "I'm excited, Sassy. Our first guests!"

"Me too. Plus, I'm excited for our furniture to arrive tomorrow," I said, giving my lower back a quick rub.

Mom saluted that statement with her coffee cup. "Any chance they'll make it here today?"

I shrugged. "I'd assume the moving company would have called me, but given the epic screw up in our delivery, maybe not."

"Well, my fingers are crossed that we get a surprise truck rolling down our driveway." Mom reached out to tap the stack of papers still on the kitchen counter. "Did you get a chance to look over the book inventory?"

"No." I glanced over at the boxes I'd piled up in the middle of the living room floor, then up at the huge hole in the ceiling. "If there are thousands of books on that list, then Len probably had the ones in the attic catalogued as well."

Going over to a box that had fallen through from the attic, I grabbed an armful of books. I doubted Lucky would probably take more than five or ten in total, and I refused to send these to the junkyard with the floral couch. I'd decided instead to put a bunch of them in the cabins with a small sign encouraging guests to take one or two or three home with them. I could also set up a free library in the office, telling guests there would be no need to return the books.

"I feel like we should continue with the book database, out of respect for the dead, you know." Mom sipped her coffee.

I couldn't tell if she was teasing or not.

"Well, that can be your project. I've got enough to do without keeping track of a thousand old books." I held one up. "I'm taking these out to the cabins."

"Make sure you snap pictures of them and send them to me," Mom said. "That way I don't have to go running all over the campground and disturbing guests to inventory their books."

I rolled my eyes, not sure why Mom was so obsessed with keeping track of these things. But if it made her happy... Taking a quick picture of each book with my cell phone, I texted the lot over to her, grabbed the ring of keys, called Elvis to come with me, and headed for the cabins.

The little tables in each cabin had a shelf at the bottom, so I stacked three additional books there, making sure there were three original ones on the top of each table. After several trips back and forth to the house for more books, I managed to empty two of the boxes that had fallen down from the attic. Feeling accomplished, I tore down the empty boxes, took them to the dumpster behind the office, then went in to finish assembling the Easter-egg hunt goodies. At noon, I got a text that Lucky had arrived and was by the owner's house. I left Mom working in the office and took Elvis with me, only to find that Lucky was actually *in* the owner's house.

My first thought was that we really needed to start locking the door during the day. The campground would be potentially hosting over eighty guests and I didn't want to discover any of them wandering around Mom's and my personal home.

My second thought was annoyance that Lucky had just strolled on in and hadn't waited for me to make the short walk over from the office. But I *had* known he was coming to look over the books. The guy was probably in a hurry to get started and get out of here. And I hated confrontation, so

I ignored what I assumed was probably just a lack of manners.

"This is it." I waved a hand at the hundreds of books still on the shelves by the fireplace. Lucky didn't seem to have brought any boxes with him, confirming that he didn't figure he'd be leaving with more than a handful.

"There are some in the cabins too?" He asked, stepping closer to eye the books on the shelf.

Ugh. Maybe I should have waited to restock the cabins. I really didn't want Lucky dragging dirt into the cabins, most of which were clean and ready for our arriving guests, so I made an executive decision.

"Don't worry about those. They're for the guests to read, so I'll just keep them." Even if he wanted one or two of those books, the fifty cents he'd pay me for them wouldn't be worth the bother of needing to tidy up the cabins once more.

He shrugged, still looking at the titles on the shelves. "I'll just see what's here then."

I stood around for a few minutes, then washed up our coffee mugs from this morning. Finally I decided that there was no sense in waiting while Lucky looked through hundreds of books. It wasn't like there was anything here for him to steal. Honestly, I'd welcome it if he absconded with the ugly couch, the broken chairs, or even the box of wrapping paper in Mom's bedroom closet. But no one wanted that stuff. Heck, I was pretty sure he wasn't even going to want any of these books. And I had work to do.

So with a mumbled explanation, I left him alone in the house and went to the garage. There I found an electrical tester, a bucket, and a wrench. Heading over to the office, I grabbed a pack of batteries off the camp store shelf for the tester.

"Mark off this pack of double-A's for me," I told Mom, who was typing away on the computer. "I'm going to go check the RV sites and make sure they've got water and electricity. If not, we're going to have to get emergency repairs done or have some unhappy guests tomorrow."

"Len Trout's boys probably winterized the place after he died," Mom reminded me. "The electric should be on, but check the breaker by the garage—there's one meter for the campsites, and cabins, and one for the house, office, garage, laundry, and bathhouses."

Shoot, I hadn't even thought of that.

"Would the water be on a separate line as well?" I wondered. The campsite was on a well, but there might be a separate water main for the campsite area. We had water in the house, office, bathhouses, and laundry, but there might be a valve I needed to open up for the camping sites.

"It might be. The only reason I know about the electric is because I called to have an account opened and the power turned on before closing. And I noticed in the business paperwork that there were two bills."

I frowned, wondering where the switch for the water might be. The house water main and the well tank were probably in the cellar—an area I hadn't even bothered to explore yet. It was only accessed through one of those slanted, double doors outside of the kitchen. I remembered from the pictures it had a dirt floor, and some rather precarious looking wooden steps.

I sincerely hoped I didn't have to go down there or spend the rest of the day figuring out how to turn the water on.

"We've got two more cabins booked with guests arriving Friday," Mom announced. "And four more RV guests are arriving Friday as well. I just answered three e-mails asking if we were open for tent camping."

From her cheerful tone, I knew she'd replied in the affirmative. And honestly, it wouldn't be a problem for us to take on tent campers right now as long as they were prepared for some cold nights. I glanced over at the shelves, thinking we might want to put out those hand and foot warming packs I'd seen in back of the storeroom. Other than that, the tent spots were mowed and cleaned up. Once Austin finished cleaning the other cabins and outbuildings, we'd be ready for business.

But I needed to make sure all the RV spots were ready to go. Once we got the urgent repairs done and both cleaning and turnover down to a well-oiled routine, then I could turn my attention to the little improvements that would keep guests coming back year after year, like painting the docks and stringing festive lights around the waterfront and the common areas. There were some Adirondack chairs behind the office that I wanted to repair and paint. They'd look nice for around the big firepit. I wanted to check and see if the soda machine by the bathhouse was actually working, and if it was, stock it. There were probably a million other little things I wasn't thinking about, but I was already back to the positive, optimistic self I'd been when I'd signed on the dotted line just three days ago.

But first things first.

I made my way to the RV section of the campground with my bucket, wrench, and electrical tester in hand. A packed dirt-and-gravel road looped off the main drive with the pads on the outside of the circle, and a grassy common area in the center. The grass had been mowed, and Austin had already filled in the worst of the potholes. I eyed the dirty metal grills, thinking that was what I'd assign my young handyman to do for the weekend. Grill cleaning duty—the ones here, at the cabins, and where the tent campers would be setting up. Yes, the docks needed to have some boards replaced, but it was still a bit cold for anyone but the most dedicated fishermen. The dock could wait a week or two, but I wanted these grills to shine—or at the very least, not look like a rusted, greasy mess.

Stopping at the first RV pad, I looked around, thinking it looked pretty sparse for what we were charging. I'd never been in an RV or camper other than the models I'd toured at the county fair. I knew they had propane tanks and a water tank, but used the campground hook-ups when parked, so maybe electric and water were the only amenities needed? Besides the grill and the picnic table, that is?

Walking over to the faucet that was sticking two feet up from the ground, I said a quick prayer and turned the handle. It made a horrible groaning noise. For a few seconds I was afraid I *would* need to call in a plumber, maybe have to dig up acres of underground piping, maybe spend thousands I didn't have on pumps and lines. Had the pipes frozen? A tree root cracked an underground section?

Brown water sputtered out of the faucet and into my bucket. I let out a relieved breath. It turned clear after a few more seconds, so I shut it off. Dumping the water from my bucket into the grass, I went to the next site, then the next, checking the water in each one. Each time the water sputtered out brown, then quickly turned clear.

As long as the RV guests had water and electricity, their essentials would be covered. Austin could clean the grills, and maybe give the picnic tables a quick check and sanding to spruce them up a bit. If I had time, I'd head into the garden shop next week and begin to add some weather-hardy annuals here and there to beautify the area. Hanging baskets would look nice on the cabins as well.

Although…I grimaced, thinking about the balance in our checking account. Guests this week would provide a nice hit of cash, but I'd spent a lot at the store already, and was going to have to spend even more on the roof repairs, the lumber for the porches and docks. Austin would need a paycheck next week. And in addition to that sagging gutter, there was now a big hole in my living room ceiling that needed patched, sanded, and painted—although that might have to wait until I our bank account had fattened up a bit. I didn't want to run us too close to empty, only to have some emergency happen at the campground and not have the funds to pay for it.

With the water tested and functioning, I walked up to the electrical box on the first site. Flipping open the lid open, I froze. A huge wasp was building a nest inside the box. It moved around, fluttering its wings as if it were about to take flight. The thing didn't have to warn me twice. I backed quickly away, prepared to drop the electrical tester and run for it if the wasp came after me.

"Is something wrong?" Lottie's voice called from behind me.

I moved sideways, so I could see her but still keep the stinging insect in my line of vision.

"There's a wasp nest in the electrical box," I told her.

"Do you need some spray? I can run back to my house and get some." She moved closer, and that's when I saw she had a baking dish in one of those carriers that kept things hot. The enticing aroma of meatloaf hit my nose.

It was good to have a friend. I liked Lottie, and that wasn't just based on her supplying us with food. She was cheerful, interesting, and kind. Yes, she had admitted to spying on us from the roof of her house with a rifle scope, but I was more than willing to overlook some quirky behavior in a friend.

"I think I saw a can of spray under the kitchen sink," I told her. "Let's go up to the house. I'll check to see if it was wasp spray or something else."

"If it's not, you can borrow some of mine," she said as we started walking back down the drive. "I always keep a can handy in the garage, and one out near the boathouse. This time of year the queens are looking for places to build a nest. I feel like I'm constantly knocking them down and spraying them. Makes me feel kind of guilty. They're essential early pollinators, you know, but I don't want a bunch of wasps swarming around me when I'm trying to get a tan out on the raft."

"Me either." I'd need to check the garage and the boathouses and docks for any nest building. The cabins and house and office too. I should probably pick up a few cans of spray next time I was in town and make a weekly sweep. It would be horrible if Mom or a guest got stung.

"Oh! I almost forgot!" Lottie laughed and held up the dish she was carrying. "I brought some meatloaf for you and your mother. I noticed your movers haven't arrived yet, and you've been so busy getting the campground ready that I wasn't sure you've had a decent meal in days. I always make a large batch to freeze, so it wasn't any bother to whip up an extra."

I absolutely overlooked that Lottie knew about the no-show movers and smiled. "That meatloaf smells amazing. Thank you so much. I picked up a pre-roasted chicken at the store the other day, but we're back to sandwiches tonight."

She shot me a sly look. "I'm assuming Jake Bailey stayed for that pre-roasted chicken as well?"

Heavens. I did not need the small-town rumor mill speculating on what was going on between me and the sometimes-deputy neighbor.

"I wanted to repay him for cutting up that tree that had fallen on the roof of cabin six," I explained. "Once we get settled in, I really want to have you and Scotty over for dinner as well."

There. Hopefully extending an invitation to Lottie and her husband would make last night's impromptu dinner with Jake seem like just a neighborly activity.

"Oh." Lottie actually blushed, squirming a little at the offer. "I'd...we'd like that. Scotty's schedule is kind of crazy, so it might just be me."

"That's fine. I'll have you both over again when his work is less hectic," I assured her, wondering why she was so flustered at the invitation.

We climbed onto the porch. I opened the door for Lottie, then came in behind her, stopping abruptly when I saw the mess that was my living room. The shelves were empty, and the books that had previously been stacked two-deep were now scattered all over the floor.

"My goodness! What happened?" Lottie exclaimed.

Lucky happened, that's what.

"Stumpy from the antique store sent Lucky over to look through my books and see if there were any they might want to buy. I didn't expect him to wreck the place." I moved a pile aside so Lottie could make it through to the kitchen.

And where *was* Lucky? His car was still out front. I glanced around, wondering for a second if he'd somehow become buried under the pile of books. Then I wondered whether he'd ignored what I'd said earlier and gone out to look at the books in the cabins. But I'd left the keys in the office with Mom, not on the hook by the door where I usually kept them. And I doubted Mom would have just handed over the ring of keys to some random guy who waltzed into the office saying he wanted to check out old books for purchase.

Just then Lucky came out from the hallway that led to the bedrooms. Had he been back there snooping? Maybe I'd been wrong to leave him unattended in the house. I might hate confrontation, but I was about to make an exception and give this man a piece of my mind.

"Sorry about the mess," he told me, bending to scoop up a

stack of books. "I had to use your bathroom, but I intended to clean all this up before I leave."

Oh. Now I felt like a jerk for thinking poorly of the man. There was only one bathroom in the house. It wasn't like I'd deny him use of it, or make him walk clear across to one of the campground bathhouses.

"Did you find anything you wanted?" I asked, helping him shove the books back on the shelves.

"Those five over there."

My heart sank. Only five? He'd dug through the entire contents of the bookshelves and only found *five* books he wanted to buy from me?

"I can give you fifty cents each," he informed me.

Great. I'd just made a whopping two dollars and fifty cents. And I still had a gazillion books I didn't know what to do with.

"Are there any romances?" Lottie called from the kitchen. "I'll take *those* off your hands for fifty cents each."

"They're all history and non-fiction and that kind of stuff," I called back, wishing that some of them were romances. Or mysteries.

"I'd like to take any other books you might have on birds or butterflies," Lucky told me. "Naturalist stuff sells pretty well at the flea markets. I'd pay you more for them."

I looked around and grabbed that hummingbird migration book I'd pulled off the shelf my first day here. "Like this?"

Something approaching excitement sparked in his eyes, only to fade as he looked at the cover. "No. I'm looking for stuff with illustrations. Like that kind of book, but with pictures."

"Well if you didn't find it here, then I don't have it," I told him, thinking that I'd keep my eyes open for something like that when I was going through the boxes in the attic. I wasn't going to put any effort into it though. Lucky's idea of paying me more was probably a dollar per book. Not enough money for me to risk falling through the attic floor again.

"I put the meatloaf in the oven to keep warm—holy macaroni, what happened to your ceiling? Was there a leak? I don't remember any rain the last few nights, though."

"I went up in the attic to look for cookware, slipped off the rafters, and fell through," I told her.

Her eyes widened. "Are you okay? I can't believe you're walking around and not in the hospital in traction."

"I didn't fall all the way through. Just my legs," I said. "I managed to hold on to one of the rafters until Jake got here to help me out."

"Were there any books up in the attic?" Lucky asked, clearly not as concerned about my physical wellbeing as Lottie was.

"Yes, but I not going up there to get them down, and neither are you right now." I waved at the remaining piles of books. "Just leave this. I'll clean it up later. I've got wasps to spray and electrical boxes to test, and I don't have any more time for books right now."

I was losing my patience with this man—but I wasn't irritated enough to turn down his two dollars and fifty cents for the five books he carried out. Just before he left, I remembered to take pictures of them to send to Mom for her revised inventory.

"What was that about?" Lottie motioned toward my phone as I texted the pictures to Mom.

"Evidently Len Trout has some complex inventory system for his book collection. Mom is keeping up with it as some sort of memorial to him, I guess. There's a stack of papers on the counter she printed out with the whole inventory. It's insane."

I looked around the kitchen counters, not seeing the

stack anywhere. They'd been here this morning, when I'd let Lucky in.

"That little weasel," I huffed, glancing out the front window to see Lucky heading down the drive. "I think he stole the papers."

Lottie laughed. "Why? Unless he thinks it'll be quicker to glance through that list than root through your attic looking for any of those bird books he wants."

"Well he could have just asked me," I griped, annoyed at the guy. "We can always print a new list off if we want. It's not like I would have said no if he'd told me he wanted to look through the list. He didn't have to sneak it out of here in his coat pocket or something."

Lottie shook her head. "Lucky Miller always was an odd duck. Not super friendly, you know. He's had a few jobs outside of Reckless, but he keeps getting fired. Each time Stumpy takes him back in and lets him work in the antique store until he finds something else."

"I can imagine someone with a sour personality and tendencies toward petty theft would have a hard time holding down a job. It's not just the book inventory papers either. Jake had said Lucky got his hand caught in a soda machine trying to steal a Mountain Dew."

As soon as I'd said it, I felt a bit ashamed. There were a lot worse things in the world than trying to get a free soda, or sneaking out some papers that weren't valuable or confidential. Lots of my coworkers had taken home pens or the occasional notepad, and I hadn't branded them as thieves. Just because Lucky wasn't the most personable guy in the world didn't mean he was a hardened criminal.

"He's really not a bad guy, just weird and lazy and kind of greedy. Besides, I don't think Lucky has the time to break into someone's home or rob a person," Lottie commented. "The only trouble he's ever been in was taking change out of the cup holders of unlocked cars on Main Street when he was a kid. He hangs out at the Twelve Gauge a lot, but he's never one of the guys who gets in fights, drives drunk, or gambles. He just kinda sits there on his own, has his beer, then heads on home."

I sighed, feeling guilty again for being angry at the man. He was just socially awkward and not a people-person. He'd made a mess of my living room, but he'd been willing to clean it up until I made him leave. He'd been back where the bedrooms were, but that *was* where the bathroom was as well. And him taking the inventory, looking it over, and letting me know what he wanted would be a whole lot easier than me rooting through boxes in the attic only to find out he didn't want any of those books. Maybe he'd meant to ask me about taking it, but hadn't had time with me practically shoving him out the door.

I needed to be more positive about how I regarded people. Not everyone was going to be my cup of tea. That didn't mean they were dishonest or that I should instantly suspect them of having bad motives.

"When Jake came over yesterday to haul me out of the ceiling, he said there had been progress in finding Daryl Butts's murderer," I told Lottie, as I began to put the books back on the shelf.

Lottie walked over to help me. "Billy Tenanball," she announced.

I bit back a smile. Of course Lottie already knew more about it than I did—probably more than everyone in town besides the sheriff.

"He runs a small engine repair shop over in Red Run," Lottie continued, "but he hangs out a lot at the Twelve Gauge. Supposedly Daryl owed him a whole lot of money."

"That's what Jake said. Evidently he was overheard threatening Daryl."

Lottie leafed through one of the books, then stuck it on a shelf. "What I don't understand is why he'd kill Daryl. He'll never collect that fifty grand on a dead man."

My mouth dropped open. "Fifty grand?" That was some serious gambling debt Daryl owed.

Lottie nodded. "Evidently Daryl had been running it up over the last few years, paying some off then losing more. I get that Billy was fed up, but why not just refuse to let Daryl play cards anymore until he was paid up? Why kill him? He'll never get the money now, and he'll end up going to jail for murder."

I thought about that for a second. "Maybe he didn't expect to kill him. Don't loan sharks break kneecaps and rough people up when they're not paying? What if Billy meant to hit him on the shoulder or arm with a bat, but missed and whacked him in the head instead?"

Lottie snorted. "Then Billy needs his eyes checked. How the heck do you miss someone's arm and hit their head instead?"

I shrugged. "Maybe he ducked? I don't know. I'm just trying to figure it out because I agree with you. It seems odd to kill someone and lose any chance at all of getting at least some of your money back. Fifty thousand dollars is a lot to write off just because you're angry with someone."

"Unless something else was going on," Lottie mused. "Maybe Billy knew there was no way he'd ever get paid. Maybe he figured the new campground owners would fire Daryl, and he wouldn't even be able to do a payment plan with no income at all."

Maybe. Either way I was glad the police had a suspect and the murder of the campground's handyman was one less thing I needed to worry about.

Lottie and I finished putting the books on the shelves. As expected, I found the wasp spray under the sink. With the can in hand, I went out to tackle the electrical boxes. Lottie and I walked down the driveway together. Lottie lingered to shout encouragement at me while I sprayed the electrical box, then carefully removed the nest.

The best news of all? There was actually an electrical current in the outlet. There was electrical current in *all* of the outlets. And I'd only had to spray three more wasp's nests.

"Join us for dinner," I offered as Lottie said her goodbyes. "I'm sure you brought enough meatloaf for an army. We've got leftover potato salad from last night, and I bought some cheeses and luncheon meat. We can have a little charcuterie before dinner, then dig in."

"Oh that sounds fun!" Lottie beamed. "Thank you. I'll definitely come for dinner."

"Bring Scotty," I suggested. Unlike me, Lottie had a husband who probably wanted to have dinner with his wife. Then I remembered what she'd said about his job. "If he's home, that is."

She blinked for a second then laughed. "Oh, he's out of town this whole week on business. It's his busy season at work, you know."

I nodded sympathetically. "I remember you said that."

"I'd love to come for dinner, though. Are you finished with that planning form you owe The Bird on Friday? If you want, we can work on it together after dinner."

"That would be great." Lottie was a local, and she clearly had her finger in every pie. Having her go over my ideas, make suggestions and giving me pointers would mean the plan would be less likely to be kicked back by The Bird for revisions. And I knew she'd share my enthusiasm for the upcoming campground events.

I watched Lottie speed walk down the driveway, thinking how wonderful it was to have a friend right next door. I wondered what sort of business her husband did where he was gone for long stretches of time like that. Sales? Long-haul truck driver?

And speaking of long-haul truck driver, there was a tractor trailer slowly making its way up the driveway.

The movers. Halleluiah, the movers had finally arrived.

CHAPTER 17

"That's not my couch," I insisted, my voice rising in volume.

"Nope. Definitely not our couch," Mom agreed.

"Are you sure?" The man scratched his head and looked at a clipboard while his coworkers continued to unload furniture that was definitely not mine.

"Don't...stop..." I waved at the moving people, as if I could somehow shoo them and the stuff back on the truck. "Yes, I'm sure. It's not mine. Put it back."

The man showed me the clipboard. The address was correct, but I wasn't Kenneth and Marisa Schwartz.

"Your computer screwed something up," I snapped, trying unsuccessfully to rein in my anger. It wasn't this man's fault he was trying to deliver someone else's household goods to my house, but he was the only one here in a position of relative authority, and I had to take my frustration out on someone.

"If we've got the Schwartz's stuff, where is ours?" Mom asked him. "Where did the Letouroux delivery end up?"

"Hang on. Let me call corporate and find out," the man told us.

He walked off to the side, getting his cell phone out. The other employees weren't putting any of the stuff they'd unloaded back in the truck, but at least they were no longer trying to walk someone else's couch through my doorway.

Although it *was* a nice couch. Far better than the one I'd been sleeping on the last few days. It was actually nicer than mine, if I were honest. The Schwartzes had good taste in furniture, and clearly a larger budget than I'd had. I envisioned Kenneth and Marisa were probably just as upset as I was right now—probably more given the amount of money they'd probably spent on the living room and the dinette set now sitting on the grass in front of my house.

Austin pulled his truck up a safe distance from the movers and hopped out, making his way over to us.

"Your stuff arrived! That's awesome!" he said with a grin.

"No, it's not awesome." I gritted my teeth, wondering if I'd ever get my furniture or if it would spend eternity roaming the country in the back of a tractor-trailer, never ever making it to the campground. This whole thing was honestly beginning to feel like a *Twilight Zone* episode.

"It's the wrong furniture," Mom explained to Austin. "The moving company got the addresses mixed up."

Austin shook his head and made a tsk sound. "That's horrible. Are you going to sue?"

I felt as if most people were overly litigious and didn't think of myself as a sue-happy person, but right now in the mood I was in, all it would take was one of those "you've got a lawyer" commercials and I'd pick up the phone.

"I'm sure it'll all be fine," Mom said, trying to soothe me as much as Austin. "The Schwartz's probably live over in Derwood, and they'll be able to get the right truck here in an hour or so."

"Canada." The man with the clipboard announced as he stuffed his cell phone back in his pocket. "Your furniture is up in Ottawa, and the Schwartz's are plenty mad about it."

"Imagine that," I drawled. Canada. My pots and pans and our clothing and beds and other stuff weren't even in the right country. As soon as these people actually managed to deliver my belongings, I was getting on the internet and posting some serious one-star reviews.

"How long do you think it will be?" Mom asked.

The man shrugged. "Four, maybe five days."

I sputtered a bit, then got out my phone and pulled up Google Maps. "No. Just…no. It's roughly a twelve-hour drive straight down Route 81 from Ottawa. Are they pulling the truck with a team of mules? Stopping for a nap every five miles? Because I can't imagine why it would take four to five days for a truck to get here from Ottawa."

The man lifted his hands. "You could pay extra for expedited service."

I stared at him, thinking that there might just be another murder here at the campground.

"The truck was supposed to arrive Monday. That's when the contract I signed said my goods would be delivered. Monday. And now you're sitting here in my driveway with someone else's furniture saying I need to pay extra to get the stuff you were supposed to deliver *two days ago?*"

The last three words came out more like a shriek than I would have liked, but I was done being patient with these people.

The man's eyes widened and he took a few steps back, digging his phone out of his pocket once more. He turned away as he dialed.

"You should sue," Austin informed me.

The boy was worrying me a bit with this line of thought.

Mom patted my shoulder. "It'll be here eventually, Sassy."

I blew out a breath. "I know. It's just the principal of the thing, Mom. I've been understanding, but now I just feel like they're taking advantage of me."

"I'll bet those Schwartz people aren't paying an expedite fee," Austin said in agreement. "Go get 'em, Ms. Sassy. Heck, if I had a CDL license, I'd go up to Ottawa and drive that truck down here myself."

There was a whole lot of logistics wrong with his idea, but I appreciated the support and his offer.

"I'll deal with the movers," I told Austin. "Why don't you get started on cleaning the other cabins and the outbuildings. The cleaning supplies are on the office porch and the keys for the cabins are there behind the counter. I'll post a list of jobs in the office in order of priority, but I think the cleaning will take you through tomorrow."

He nodded. "Will do, Ms. Sassy."

Austin headed off to the office, and I watched as another truck pulled down the gravel drive, parking near the cabins to the right of the house. Sadly, it was not another tractor-trailer miraculously transported from Ottawa, but a work truck loaded with ladders and building supplies.

"The roofers!" Mom exclaimed. "I'll meet with them and get the estimate. Don't let this moving company get you so upset, Sassy. It'll all work out."

I nodded, knowing she was right, but determined to stand my ground on this. Two days late on a delivery was bad enough, but six, potentially seven? That was ridiculous.

The man hung up and walked back, eyeing me nervously. "I called corporate and they agreed to waive the expedite fee. I can't guarantee you delivery tomorrow, but it shouldn't be any later than Friday."

Shouldn't be. Those two words made this statement a whole lot less reassuring, but I didn't have much choice at this point. They had my stuff. In Canada.

"Friday," I told him. "If it's not here by Friday, then I expect a full refund. And if I don't get it, I'm going to talk to a lawyer."

I winced a little as I said it, but maybe Austin was right and it was time to throw the "L" word around.

The man nodded, then waved for his crew to load the Schwartz's furniture back into the truck. I doubt my threat meant anything to him. He was just some poor employee who probably didn't make enough money to have to deal with my wrath. He probably just wanted to get out of here as quickly as possible, and didn't care one bit whether I sued his employer or not. I'd been an employee in the middle many times, so I stood back and didn't take my frustration out on him any further. If the truck wasn't here by tomorrow night, I'd call corporate myself and make my threats.

My anger faded as I watched the huge truck slowly head back down the drive, leaving exhaustion in its place. Mom was right, I really had worked myself to the bone since we'd arrived here. Austin was taking care of the cleaning. Mom was dealing with the roofing estimate. There was nothing else I could do to speed up the delivery of my household goods, and everything was prepped and ready for our unexpected influx of early-spring guests tomorrow.

I should just relax for the rest of the afternoon. Dinner was in the oven, courtesy of Lottie. Maybe I'd sprawl out on the couch, read about hummingbird migration and pet Elvis. Tonight I'd have a nice dinner, then Lottie and I would go over the summer festival plans I'd put together with a cup of coffee in hand.

Taking Elvis inside the house, I grabbed the book and was just ready to make good on that promise I'd made myself to relax when I realized there was something I really did need to do first.

Laundry.

I hadn't packed a lot of clothing since the movers were supposed to be here the day after we arrived. Right now my jeans were on their second day of use, with another pair even dirtier in a pile with shirts, underwear, and socks in the corner of my bedroom. I really didn't have to wear dirty clothing for another day—or possibly two. So instead of relaxing on the couch, I grabbed the pile of clothes and headed for the amenities building closest to the owner's house. I could throw everything in the washer, then go back and read a bit while the machine did its thing. Mixing rest with laundry was close enough to relaxation, right?

I sorted my lights and darks into two machines, checking the pockets on my jeans to make sure I wasn't sending any keys or business cards through the wash. Sure enough, there was a crumpled piece of paper in one of the pockets. I pulled it out and opened it up to read the scribbled text written in black ink.

"Hoskins Used Books," I said, frowning at the number. Where the heck had I gotten this?

Then it hit me. Cabin five. I'd found it on the floor that night when Elvis had dragged me halfway across the campground after I'd seen what I thought was a light, and he'd smelled something.

I wondered who had dropped it. Maybe one of Len Trout's sons had been thinking of unloading all the books in the house after all. Either the store hadn't wanted them, or I'd bought the campground before they could arrange anything, and just left it all here for me to deal with.

Shoving the paper into the pocket of the jeans I was currently wearing, I vowed to give them a call. It wouldn't hurt to see if they wanted any of these books. Maybe I'd get lucky and this time I'd make more than two dollars and fifty cents off the deal.

I'd definitely call them. But not today. The rest of today was for relaxation. Hoskins Used Books could wait until tomorrow.

CHAPTER 18

"**N**ot again," I mumbled, trying to muffle Elvis's low-pitched growls with one of the sofa pillows.

In spite of the laundry, I did actually manage to rest this afternoon. In fact, the hummingbird migration book actually put me to sleep, and for that short nap, I was grateful. But a thirty-minute nap wouldn't help if I continued to have my sleep each night disturbed by Elvis worrying over the local wildlife.

"Oh for Pete's sake." I made a growl that matched Elvis's as I rolled off the couch and made my way over to where he stood with his nose pressed against the window. "What's wrong? Is it another raccoon?"

I looked out the window and didn't see anything. Elvis growled once more and I hesitated, undecided as to whether I should go out and look, or try to go back to sleep and hope my dog eventually gave up and did the same.

He growled again, then inexplicably began to wag his tail.

"Fine. I'll go check, but you're staying here," I told him. I really didn't feel like having my arm nearly ripped out of its socket tonight, and I didn't want to keep rewarding the hound's behavior by a nice little midnight walk-and-sniff every time he growled at the window.

Pocketing my phone, I threw my coat on over my pajamas. I also grabbed the broom from beside the door, thinking it might serve to shoo a raccoon away from the dumpster, or even as a makeshift weapon, just in case I needed to defend myself against any wild animals. Not that a broom would be much good against a bear, but I didn't really expect to encounter anything larger than a squirrel or another raccoon.

"You stay," I told Elvis in a firm voice. Then I went outside and stood on the porch for a moment to let my eyes adjust.

It was a cloudless night, but the moon was waning. The faint glow from the light above the shower house door didn't do much to illuminate the campground. Hefting my broom a bit, I stepped off the porch and looked around. All was silent, the cabins hulking shadows to my right and left, the lake glistening faintly in the moonlight behind the house. Glancing back, I saw Elvis at the window, staring at me intently, his tail slowly wagging.

I circled the house and saw nothing—not even a mouse scampering around. Feeling brave, and now wide-awake, I decided to head to the office and make sure the coffee pot was set up and ready to start auto-brewing at six. After tonight, I'd really need a cup of coffee—or even four—in the morning.

As I came along the right side of the house, I saw something move from the corner of my eye. I froze and watched a shadow move along the porch of cabin one.

Cabin one wasn't more than fifty yards from where I stood, so I could clearly see that this shadow was a person, not a raccoon, and absolutely not a bear. I shivered for a second, wondering if I was seeing a ghost, but then it tugged on the cabin door, put something in its pocket, and hopped off the porch with the what I believed were very un-ghostly-like movements.

I couldn't move. I could barely breathe. There was an intruder on my property. We had no guests tonight, and there was no reason whatsoever for someone to be here after midnight, going in or out of cabin one—or any of the buildings.

My thoughts raced a million miles an hour. Was this the murderer? But why would Billy Tenanball come back here? Returning to the scene of his crime when he was the prime suspect of a murder investigation would be an incredibly stupid thing to do, and I couldn't think of one reason why this late-night visit would be worth the risk. A robber? That was a ludicrous idea. There was nothing here to steal. Maybe it was that vagrant the 911 operator had mentioned, trying to find a cozy cabin to spend the night. If so, I needed to get my feet a-moving, get back inside the house, and call the police, because I wasn't about to confront this person—especially not with a broom as my only means of self-defense.

Staring at the shadow, I slowly backed up, mentally calculating how close I was to the porch, and if I could make it inside before the intruder caught me. Deciding to make a break for it, I spun around and saw a person crouched down behind one of the shrubs.

With a scream that came out more like a squawk, I swung the broom around, handle-end first. The person leapt upright, and the blow that should have hit them in the head landed instead on their waist, partially deflected by a quick pivot and their right arm.

The person grabbed the broom handle and let out a soft curse. I recognized the voice before he spoke.

"Sassy," Jake hissed. "It's me."

Oh, thank God! Relief almost brought me to my knees. I

wasn't outside alone, facing two intruders armed with only a broom, I was outside facing one intruder with a sometimes-deputy. I liked those odds much better. In fact, I'd like them a whole lot better if I went back inside and let Jake deal with this on his own.

"There's someone on the porch of cabin one," I hissed, turning around to realize that the shadow on the porch of cabin one was gone and nowhere to be seen.

"I know." He let go of the broom and rubbed his waist. "You always swing first and ask questions later? What if I'd been your mother?"

"My mother wouldn't have been lurking behind a bush in the middle of the night," I told him, still a bit shaky. "She would have walked right up and yelled 'Sassy, what are you doing out here?'" I suddenly felt a little guilty about whacking him with the broom handle. "Are you okay?"

"Better than I would be if you'd whacked me in the head like you obviously intended," he answered, his amused tone telling me that he hadn't suffered a real injury, except perhaps to his pride.

"Who was that?" I pointed over to the cabin. "The sheriff? Another deputy? Crime scene techs?"

I doubted any of those people would be sneaking around the cabin at night—at least without calling or informing me that they'd be there. I guess part of me hoped there was an innocent explanation to this whole thing that wouldn't cause me to lose sleep at night thinking of intruders and murderers.

"No." Jake sighed and ran a hand through his hair. "If you hadn't been out here, roaming around in your pajamas with a broom, I might have been able to find out who it was and maybe even arrest him."

"If you had told me you were planning on patrolling my campground and that you'd be sneaking around the bushes in the middle of the night, then maybe I would have stayed in the house," I shot back. "Why *are* you here?"

For someone who'd always disliked confrontation, I sure was getting good at it.

I shivered, wrapping my arms around my waist. "Come in to the office for a cup of coffee," I offered. "I'm too wired to sleep right now, and it's too cold to have this discussion outside."

Jake nodded. "Guess I could use a cup of coffee. And I probably do owe you an explanation."

We headed over to the office. I unlocked the door, turned on the lights, and got the industrial-sized pot of coffee going, while Jake looked around.

"I've never been in here before. This is real cute. I like the little bags of toiletries you put together for sale. Was that your idea, or something Len had before?"

"It was my idea." I pulled two mugs off the shelf. "Len sold the sample-sized stuff individually, but I thought a packet would be a good idea. Flora from The Coffee Dog is going to be making daily deliveries with hiker snack packs, and any bagged breakfasts or lunches people order the day before. They'll be stocking our shelves with fresh ground coffee on consignment, too."

He made his way over to the refrigerator unit. "Drinks. Cheeses and hummus. Bait. I saw the fishing poles outside. Are you going to be renting those?"

I shook my head. "I'm not an expert—heck, I'm not even an amateur—but those poles look like something Len picked up at a yard sale. People can buy bait, but the poles will be free for any guest to use. I figure if someone's serious about fishing, they probably will have brought their own gear."

"True." Jake opened the door and looked at a few of the containers of bait before shutting it. "There was always good fishing from the piers here. And you've got that boat launch by the dock, you know. It's probably overgrown, but it's there. Len had a pontoon boat and a bass boat with an outboard. They might need some work, but I'll bet they're both sound. I doubt his sons hauled them away."

"I'm realizing Len's sons didn't haul *anything* away," I drawled. The idea of boats was intriguing. If the boats were still here, they were probably locked up in either the garage or one of the other buildings I hadn't even gotten around to checking yet. Of course, I had no idea how to repair one. Or drive one. I wasn't even sure how to start a boat.

"Yeah. I think Len's sons were kind of overwhelmed. It's hard when parents leave a whole bunch of stuff behind—especially stuff you don't really know what to do with. It feels kinda disrespectful to just haul it all off to the dump."

I agreed. That was my dilemma with the books. The couch and other old stuff I was fine with trashing, if breaking a mirror might earn me seven years of bad luck, then sending a thousand books to the dump might earn me a lifetime.

Jake continued to browse the items I had for sale while I poured the coffee.

"What's this?" he asked.

I turned to see him pointing to the egg decorating kits I had lined up on a table.

"Activities for this week's campers. Egg decorating that I'm hoping adults as well as kids will enjoy. An egg hunt with candy in plastic eggs. And a Peep diorama contest for Friday night's bonfire."

He picked up a package of Peeps. "You know, I actually like these things."

I laughed, feeling much better than I had fifteen minutes ago. "Well, you're the only one. Here, take your coffee, have a seat, and tell me what's going on that a sometimes-deputy is prowling around my campground after midnight."

He did as I said and I plopped down in the chair across from him.

"Well, first off, I *was* a bit concerned that maybe you did have a bear coming around the campsite. It's that time of year when young males are out looking for territory and some garbage cans to raid. I didn't think you'd be equipped to handle a bear on your own."

I leaned back in the chair, my eyebrows rising. "And *you* can handle a bear on your own?"

He chuckled. "No. But I could scare one off, then contact the park service to ask for a relocation. Of the bear, I mean. Not me. Usually if people make enough noise, they go try their luck somewhere with less hassle, but occasionally the rangers need to dart one and move him deeper into the woods where he's less likely to be harassing hikers, livestock, dogs—"

"Campers," I finished for him. "But that was no bear I saw tonight. I'm getting the impression that it wasn't a bear snooping around the cabins the last few either."

"I'm thinking the same." Jake took a quick sip of coffee, then continued. "Oliver took Billy Tenanball down to the station last night and locked him up pending charges. Billy claims he's innocent. I mean, people always say they're innocent, that some other guy did it, but I had a weird feeling about this. This morning I looked over Oliver's notes on the case, including the interview with Billy. Daryl owed him fifty thousand dollars in gambling debt. I gotta say it doesn't speak well to Billy's intelligence that he kept giving Daryl credit to the point where the man owed that much money. Anyone with a brain in their head knows Daryl couldn't come up with that much money if he had a lifetime to pay it off."

I nodded, remembering that Lottie had told me about the gambling debts. "But wouldn't eventually getting *some* money out of Daryl be better than none at all? Why kill him when you might at least be able to get a few thousand out of him a year and not be facing murder charges?"

"That's definitely a sticking point in the case," Jake pointed out. "Billy claims Daryl said he was going to have the money for him in a few weeks. The day before you found Daryl dead in one of your cabins, Daryl supposedly met up with Billy at the Twelve Gauge and told him he was coming into some money, that he could pay Billy what he owed him in full."

I eyed Jake over the edge of my coffee cup. "How in the world could Daryl come up with fifty thousand dollars in a few weeks? Did a rich uncle pass away? Did he win the lottery? Find a leprechaun?"

"Nope, nope, and nope. But I did think about the campground. Sometimes when people pass away, rumors get started about them having money stashed in mattresses or buried in coffee cans out back. Made me wonder if Daryl didn't think there was something here. Like there were riches just waiting for him to dig them up."

I thought about his theory for a second. "That's a pretty big reach. Were there rumors in town about Len having money buried in the backyard somewhere? Billy could just be lying. Or Daryl could have lied to Billy to stall for time. Maybe Daryl planned to skip town the next day and hoped Billy would never find him."

"Maybe. I can see Daryl telling Billy he'll have the money for him in a week or two then skipping town." Jake sighed and leaned back in his chair. "Either way, I think we've got a shaky motive as far as this case goes, no weapon, no real proof. Half the town wouldn't have an alibi for the window of time when we think Daryl was killed. I've got no crystal ball on what the prosecutor is going to decide about this one, but if I did, I'd be predicting we're going to have to let

Billy go until we can build a better case with more evidence."

I blew out a breath, not sure how I felt about that. I wanted Daryl's murderer behind bars, but didn't want to see someone charged for murder if they weren't the killer.

"I got to thinking that if Billy didn't kill Daryl, then someone else did," he went on. "If Daryl actually believed there was a metaphorical pot of gold buried on the property, maybe he'd told someone else about it—someone who could help him dig it up, or help him sell it once he got his hands on it. And maybe this person thought to take Daryl out of the equation and not share the profits."

"I assume if the killer has been prowling around here for the last three out of four nights, that means he stupidly killed his partner before he knew exactly where the pot of gold was hidden. Or buried." I shivered at the thought that a murderer had been prowling around so close to where Mom and I were sleeping.

"Fifty thousand dollars is a lot of money," Jake commented. "Especially here in Reckless. That kind of money makes people a little crazy, makes them do rash things that they normally wouldn't do."

"If Daryl had a partner that he was going to cut in on the deal, whatever pot of gold they were going to dig up was probably worth *more* than fifty grand," I mused. "Maybe seventy thousand. Maybe a hundred thousand."

"People have been killed for less," Jake said as he stood. "Which is why I'm going to recommend you stay locked in your house at night until we find this killer. No more going out to investigate strange noises or lights, even if you take Elvis with you."

I stood as well. "If I see anything, I'll call you."

He nodded grimly. "You won't need to call me. Until we

catch this guy, I'll be here, watching and waiting. So don't try to bean me with a broom handle or anything, okay?"

I smiled, reassured that he'd be guarding my campground while I slept—from bears as well as murderers.

"I'll stay inside. And I won't hit you with a broom handle again." I lifted a hand. "I promise."

CHAPTER 19

Reckless Neighbors App:
Pickleball teams are full for this summer! If you missed out, you can still watch us play and cheer us on to win against our Savage rivals. No more free alewives, but you can purchase your own at Bait and Beer.

Is someone missing a cow? I have a black and white heifer on my front lawn. She came down Main Street about six this morning. Hurry before she decides the grass is greener elsewhere and moves on. Right now she's breakfasting at Main and Mulberry.

I was up early, taking Elvis for a quick walk and doing a sweep of the area in preparation for our guests. I didn't see any signs of Jake, and assumed he'd gone back home when the sun had come up to take care of his horses and get some sleep.

Last night's events and my conversation with Jake had unnerved me. Even with the sometimes-deputy guarding the campground at night, I didn't truly feel safe. What if the killer came back during the day? And we had guests arriving this afternoon. How would Jake be able to tell the difference between the killer and one of the campers walking to the bathhouse for a midnight pee? And what was the killer looking for? What could Len Trout possibly have of value here that would drive someone to murder?

I was convinced that Daryl had made the whole thing up, fabricated some pot-of-gold tale to get Billy off his back for a few weeks. But the killer obviously didn't know that if they were still looking for the cash or gold or whatever.

Trying to put the whole thing out of my mind and instead concentrate on things that were actually within my sphere of control, I grabbed a cup of coffee, collected my laundry from the dryer, and headed back to the house. Mom got up soon after I was done folding and putting away my meager wardrobe, and we breakfasted on leftovers while Elvis ate his kibble.

Mom headed to the office with Elvis in tow, saying she planned to park there for the day so she could check in guests and get them situated. I putted around the house a bit, full of anxious energy and ready for the first round of campers to arrive. With nothing to do for now, I eyed the hole in my ceiling. It would be a perfect time to go up to the attic and sort through some of the boxes, but I didn't want to risk falling again—especially with no one here to help me. As loyal as Elvis was, I doubted the dog would be of much assistance beyond barking at my legs dangling from the ceiling.

Glancing over at the books Lottie and I had haphazardly stuck back on the shelves, I remembered the balled-up bit of paper I'd picked up from cabin five with the phone number for Hoskins Used Books on it.

A used bookseller. In Virginia, judging from the area code. Maybe I could unload enough of these books to at least pay for the ceiling repair. Or dinner at the Chat-n-Chew.

Books. I frowned, wondering if that was the buried treasure Daryl had been referring to. I shook my head, laughing a bit at my train of thought. Why would Daryl have ever thought these books were worth anything, let alone fifty thousand dollars or more? Had Len hinted to him that he had a Gutenberg Bible in among all these fifty-cent tomes? Or maybe I was just letting my imagination get away from me.

Only one way to find out. I grabbed my phone, dialed the store, and asked for the name on the card.

"Elton Hoskins," a man's voice intoned.

I was a bit embarrassed about even calling this guy. He probably had no idea how his number ended up in one of my cabins, or even where Reckless, Virginia, was, but it was worth a shot.

"I've got a weird question," I said.

He sighed. "We don't sell porn. Not even vintage porn. There's a place in New York I can refer you to, though."

"I don't want porn," I told him. "I'm looking to sell some old books. Most of them are hardback and they seem to be all non-fiction. They're about things like the history of haberdashery and hummingbird migration. Stuff like that."

"We might be interested. If it's ten or twenty books, you can always bring them in to our store in Richmond."

I winced. "I'm guessing it's close to a thousand books."

He sucked in a breath. "Do you have an inventory list you can send me? That's probably easier."

It would be. I scribbled down the e-mail address he gave me and made a note to send him a copy of the inventory.

"I've got another question, that's even more weird," I continued. "And no, it's not about porn. My name is Sassafras Letouroux and I own a campground in Reckless, Virginia. I found a piece of paper in one of my cabins with your company's name and phone number, and I was wondering if you've been in contact with anyone here?

Maybe they thought they had a valuable book or something? Does the name Daryl Butts ring a bell?"

He was silent a moment. "Is that the guy with the Audubon book? I didn't get his name. He called about five or six days ago and told me he had a first edition Birds of America. I told him to send me pictures of the book, front and back and the spine as well as the copyright page, and if it was printed in 1827, then we had a deal. If he had an 1827 first edition, then I'd pay him two hundred grand for it. I never heard from him again, which isn't surprising. People call all the time thinking they've got a million-dollar book in their grandmother's attic or something, and it turns out to be a book worth five bucks at a flea market."

I cleared my throat. "Two hundred thousand? Dollars? As in two hundred thousand dollars?"

He laughed. "It's not a Gutenburg Bible, but one did fetch quite a lot at auction back in 2010."

Two hundred thousand. That would pay for the roof repair, the ceiling repair, boat repairs, *all* the repairs. I could have a pool put in for guests. A putt-putt course. I thought of all the books on the shelves, the boxes in the attics, the books in the cabins.

Oh no. The cabins. Was that why someone had been nosing around the cabins? Were they looking for this book? Had this been why Daryl had been murdered?

"Technically the book is an eight volume set," the man continued. "But any one of them is worth a lot. There are some other bird books that are in high demand by collectors as well, so if you happen to come across anything by Gould, or any illustrated book printed in the nineteenth century, give me a call."

"But the man said he had an Audubon?" I scrambled for some paper, writing down the details.

"Yeah. But like I said, a lot of people get all excited

thinking they've got a valuable book or painting or vase, only to find out it's a copy or not exactly what they'd hoped." The man laughed again. "But just in case, I'm always happy to take a look. Send me pictures, and if there's a chance it's valuable, I'll drive down to see it."

"Thanks. I'll do that." I hung up and stared at my notes. Then I grabbed the stack of papers from the kitchen counter —the newly printed inventory of books that Mom had brought in last night—and started reading.

Half an hour later, I was staring at an entry that clearly informed me *Birds of America* by John James Audubon was on the shelf beside the fireplace. Left side. Four shelves from the top.

Except Lucky had taken all the books off the shelves when he'd gone through them, and Lottie and I had just stuck them back wherever. I frantically started pulling books off the shelves, setting them carefully aside because I'd just learned that one of them might end up being worth a fortune.

After going through all the books on the shelves, I panicked, thinking that it might have been one of the books that Lucky had bought for fifty cents. Grabbing my phone, I scrolled through the pics, grateful that I'd taken the time to snap them before he'd left.

My shoulders slumped with relief when I realized it wasn't among the ones Lucky had taken. It must be in the cabins. Oh no. That's where the murderer had been searching. What if he'd already found the book and sold it? We'd never catch the killer, and I'd never get that two hundred thousand dollars.

I grabbed the set of keys off the ring by the door and dashed out of the house, noticing that there were several campers parked on the pads with people leveling their mobile living spaces and setting up. Crossing my fingers that none of the cabin guests had arrived yet, I ran for cabin one and began my search.

An hour later, I was absolutely stumped. It wasn't there. I hadn't been able to find the book anywhere. Defeated, I headed back to the house, convinced that the killer must have already found and stolen it.

Speaking of theft, that Daryl Butts was *not* getting a memorial tree. Or a plaque. I understood that gambling was an addiction and that he'd been in a real jam owing a huge sum of money, but that didn't excuse stealing from the campground. Although the guy probably hadn't thought twice about it. Len had died. His sons had abandoned all this stuff and were clearly leaving it for whoever bought the campground to deal with. He probably figured he didn't owe Len's sons anything, *or* me anything. He probably figured I'd just throw all this stuff out when I got here, and him stealing it was no different from him snatching the book out of a dumpster.

Who *was* the murderer? Had Daryl confided in someone, like Jake suspected, and that person killed him so he wouldn't have to share the money? It really didn't seem plausible for the killer to be Billy Tenanball when he'd only been a few short weeks from getting his money—unless Billy had decided he wanted the whole two hundred thousand instead of just the fifty Daryl owed him.

Why hadn't Daryl called the bookstore man back when he'd found the book? He knew it was here. Why didn't he send pictures over and arrange to get his money? Why bother to involve a partner when he didn't have to.

As I walked up the porch to my house, everything suddenly made sense.

The guy at the bookstore hadn't known Daryl's name, because it wasn't Daryl that had called, it was the partner, the killer. The killer was the one who'd dropped the paper in cabin five when he'd been searching for the book there. *That's* why Daryl had needed a partner. It was because he hadn't the foggiest idea where to sell a rare book. In fact, if Daryl had thought he had a possibly valuable old book to sell, he would probably do the same thing I'd done and gone to Stumpy's to see if they'd buy it.

Stumpy's. Lucky had gone through every book on those shelves, but been keenly interested in other books I might have elsewhere—books on nature, especially bird books with illustrations. There'd been no intruder the night before he'd come out to go through the books, because why risk an attempted burglary charge when I'd invited him in, absolutely clueless about what might be sitting on my bookshelf. And when he'd left without the prize he'd come to find, he'd returned last night, searching once more. I'd told him I'd taken books off the shelf and put them in the cabins. He'd stolen the inventory list. He'd known the book was supposed to be on the shelf. So the only other place it could be was in one of the cabins.

I threw open the door and went to the kitchen, planning on grabbing the paper, the inventory list, and calling Jake. I hadn't even made it to the counter when someone grabbed me from behind, jabbing something sharp into my back.

"Where is it?" Lucky hissed into my ear.

"I...I don't have much money, but there's probably a twenty in my purse over there. And my credit cards." I tried to stall, to act like I didn't know what he was talking about. In reality, I was on the verge of panic. This man had already killed one person. He wouldn't hesitate to kill me—especially when he discovered I had no idea where the book was.

Wait. If Lucky was the killer and had been the one searching the cabins, then why didn't *he* have the book? Why was he here threatening to stab me and not halfway to Richmond with his prize? If he didn't have the book, then where the heck was it?

"The book." I felt the point of the knife pressing through my shirt into my skin. "The bird book. Audubon's *Birds of America*. Where did you hide it?"

"You went through all the books," I told him. "Maybe it's in the attic? I don't know where it is."

He tightened his arm around me. "Don't lie. It was supposed to be on the shelf, but it wasn't. And it wasn't in the books you took to the cabins either. You hid it somewhere. Tell me where it is."

"You killed Daryl," I said, figuring if I was going to die, at least I'd get a confession out of him first. "He needed money to pay his gambling debts and came to you at the antique store to see if any of these books were worth anything."

"He wasn't as stupid as everyone thought. Len had showed him the book one time, told him it was worth some money. When Billy started coming down hard on Daryl for those debts, he looked it up on the internet and came to me, offering to sell it for fifty grand."

"But you knew it was worth more than that," I said, stalling for time and hoping someone would come to rescue me. Not Mom. Not Lottie. I really needed Jake, preferably with a gun.

Lucky laughed. "Daryl knew it was more than that too, but he didn't want too many people asking questions about why a handyman with a gambling problem managed to come across a book worth millions. He just wanted enough to pay off his debts, and knew working at an antique store, I'd be in a better position to say we'd bought it at an estate sale or something."

"Are you sure he actually had it?" I asked, an idea suddenly crossing my mind. "Maybe Daryl lied. No one's seen it. For all you know, Len's sons took it and never removed it from their father's inventory. If Len had pointed it out to Daryl as valuable, his sons probably knew about it as well."

"He sent me a picture of it," Lucky snapped. "He even sent a picture of the inside where it had the copyright info. I told him I'd give him fifty grand for it and met him in that cabin to do the exchange."

"You didn't have the money," I realized. "You were going to kill Daryl and steal the book, but after you killed him, you realized he didn't have the book on him either. He hadn't trusted you. He didn't bring the book along, wanting to wait until after he had the money to give it to you. But you killed him and then you had no idea where the book was."

"I didn't mean to kill him." Lucky's voice rose in pitch to almost a squeak. "I just meant to knock him out. Then I saw he hadn't brought the book with him, and that he was dead. I got worried someone might come, that he might have arranged for another person to meet us or check on him, so I grabbed his keys and left, thinking I'd search for the book later. I didn't realize you'd be moving in the next day."

My brain whirred, trying to think of how I was going to get out of this. It could be hours before someone came to the house.

I was just going to have to bluff—and pray.

"I hid it in the garage," I told him. "I'll show you where it is, just don't kill me. You can take the book, leave me unharmed and I won't say anything."

He hesitated. I felt the knife dig into my side a bit, felt a warm trickle where the blade had broken the skin. I knew he was trying to decide whether to kill me now or not. But he'd killed Daryl too soon and never found out where the book was hidden. He was clearly worried about the same thing happening to me.

"I'll show you where it is," I repeated. "Just don't hurt me."

I think what ultimately worked in my favor was that I was a slim-built woman of almost sixty years. He outweighed me by about fifty pounds. He had the advantage. And he had a knife.

"Okay. We're going to walk there. Don't try anything, or I'll stab you."

I nodded, then let him maneuver me around and push me toward the door. Once we were outside, he gave me a bit of space, the knife leaving my side. I had no illusions of safety, though. The guy was fast, and in less than a second he could have that knife jammed right between my ribs.

We walked over to the garage, my mind whirring as I wondered how I was going to get out of this alive. In my peripheral vision, I saw the RV campers milling about their sites, a few cars parked by the office. One of those cars I recognized as Lottie's.

Oh no. Please don't let anyone else get hurt, or get me into a hostage situation where I end up being the victim in a murder/suicide.

"Keep moving," Lucky hissed, stepping back a few feet as I pulled the keys from my pocket.

I unlocked the garage door, swinging it open and stepping just inside the threshold.

"Hi, Sassy! Happy Opening-Day! I brought over some— oh hey, Lucky."

Lottie sounded like she was only ten or so feet behind us. I saw Lucky turn at her voice. Grabbing the wrench off a workbench inside the door, I spun around and threw it at him. He dove forward with the knife, so I slammed the door shut on his arm. He howled in pain. The knife dropped, and I scooped it up, yelling for Lottie to run as the door bounced open again.

I should have known better. Lottie did no such thing. Instead she darted forward and swung the bottle of wine she was holding, clocking Lucky upside the head. He went down hard, knocked unconscious by a bottle of what looked to be a nice red blend.

"Oh wow. Didn't even break the bottle," Lottie cheerfully informed me. "I've got no idea what Lucky did or was planning to do, but should I call the police?"

I looked down at Lucky, his knife still in my one hand and adrenaline surging through me.

"I'll call them." Hopefully Shelly wouldn't give me a bunch of grief this time before sending someone out. Actually, it might be a better idea if I just called Jake directly.

"Good." Lottie held the wine bottle up like it was a club. "I'll sit on him, just in case he wakes up. Or maybe I can duct tape him. I've got some duct tape in my purse here."

Of course she did. I laughed, because in spite of the near-death experience, this suddenly all seemed funny. My mother and I owned a campground. There'd been one, almost two, murders here this week. There might be a book somewhere lying around that was worth hundreds of thousands—maybe even millions—of dollars. And my new best friend was sitting on an unconscious murderer, brandishing a wine bottle, and instructing me how to duct-tape him.

$\mathcal{M}$om and I sat at the table, sharing the wine that had saved my life, along with the woman who'd saved my life. Lottie hadn't hesitated to whack Lucky upside the head, and while that sort of thing should have bothered me, it didn't. I was grateful for my plucky friend with her spying rifle scope and her accuracy with a wine bottle. The pair of us had duct taped Lucky like a Halloween mummy, then Lottie had sat on him as I called 911. It had probably been a bit overkill, but we hadn't wanted to take our chances he'd somehow manage to break free of an entire roll of duct tape.

The duct tape held. When Lucky regained consciousness he'd been on his best behavior, no doubt more worried about Lottie and her wine bottle than our makeshift restraints. Shelly didn't give me any grief this time, and this time the sheriff himself arrived to take Lucky into custody. Evidently nearly getting stabbed warrants actual law enforcement intervention.

Thankfully none of the guests seemed to notice the commotion over by the garage, and although the sheriff's arrival garnered a few looks, everyone went back to the business of their vacations. I was hoping this meant I could keep it all hush-hush—well, as hush-hush as anything could be in a small town like Reckless.

"Do you need to go to the hospital?" Lottie asked, pointing to the bloodstain around the tear in my shirt.

"Not until after I finish my wine," I joked. "It's just a scratch," I added as Mom started to make a fuss, demanding I take off my shirt so she could see if I needed stitches. "Really, Mom. I'm fine. I'll slap some antibiotic cream on it and a bandage once I'm done with my wine."

"What in the world was that horrible man doing here?" Mom asked, returning to her seat. After the sheriff arrived and she'd discovered my near-death experience, she'd hung a sign on the office telling guests to come here so she too could have a quick glass of wine to "settle her nerves."

"Trying to stab Sassy, that's what," Lottie said. "And here I'd just told her that Lucky was harmless outside of some minor petty crime. I'd always thought I was a decent judge of character, but now I'm second guessing that."

"He was looking for a valuable book." I told the pair of them about the Audubon book, Daryl's scheme to get money to pay off his gambling debts, and Lucky's greed turning him into a murderer—almost a two-time murderer.

"I've got no idea where the book is," I added with a shrug. "The inventory says it was on the shelf by the fireplace, but it's not there. It's not in any of the cabins. Lucky didn't have it. Maybe Daryl hid it in his house or somewhere else, because I certainly can't find it."

"Audubon?" Mom frowned. "With bird illustrations? I've got it back in my bedroom under the air mattress. Sometimes I wake up in the middle of the night and can't sleep, so I grabbed it off the shelf the first night we arrived, thinking it might make a good insomnia book."

My mouth fell open. "You have it? Under your mattress?"

Mom nodded. "How much is it supposed to be worth?"

"A fortune." I got up and bolted for the back bedroom, returning with the book carefully cradled in my hands. Mom had moved over to the computer, with Lottie standing over her shoulder. I went to them, setting the book carefully down on the desk and gently opening it.

"When was it printed?" Mom asked, typing the book information into the search bar.

"1827." I frowned, looking at the date closer.

"That would make it a first edition." Mom didn't sound very excited about that. In fact she was frowning too, looking back and forth between the book and her screen.

"I think…it looks like someone inked over the date," Lottie said, her finger hovering right over the copyright and print information.

"I know." I blew out a breath, disappointed that this wasn't a two-hundred thousand dollar book after all. "I think the original date was 1927, but someone tried to make the nine into an eight. The font doesn't match the same of any of the other eights, and the ink is a bit darker."

Had the attempted forgery been done before Len had bought the book? Maybe the former campground owner really had thought the book was a first edition, although I couldn't imagine why he would have stuck such a valuable book up on the shelf next to ones worth fifty cents. It was probably more likely that Len had mentioned to Daryl that if the book had been printed a hundred years before it would have been worth a fortune, and the handyman, desperate to pay off his gambling debts, changed the date in hopes of making some quick money.

"A professional would have caught that," Lottie pointed out.

She was right. The man in Richmond would have known

right away, but Lucky wouldn't have. He'd worked at his dad's antique shop, but wasn't an expert. No, he was just a greedy thief who'd almost been conned out of fifty thousand dollars by Daryl Butts.

"A professional would have caught more than that," Mom said. "It's not just the date that's a problem. The first edition book? The one that's worth millions? It's huge. The books in that set are each three feet by two feet in size."

I peeked over her shoulder at the image she'd pulled up. A woman and a man were standing by a glass case holding a truly giant book, open to a picture of an Autumnal Warbler. The book on the desk in front of me was about nine inches by thirteen inches.

"Too bad," Lottie said, patting me on the shoulder. "If it had been a million-dollar book, we would have been celebrating with more than just this red blend."

"Daryl was trying to con Lucky out of money with a forgery, and Lucky was going to steal the book and take all the profits, but ended up accidentally killing Daryl." I shook my head in amazement over the foolishness of it all. "A man died over this book that's probably worth about five bucks. *I* almost died over this book that's worth about five bucks."

"But you didn't die." Mom closed out the internet tab and stood. "We're not suddenly rich, but you're safe and alive. That's the blessing in all this."

It was a blessing. I was safe and alive thanks to Lottie and her wine bottle. And there was so much more to be thankful for. I'd bought the campground of my dreams. We had guests, friends, and a new life ahead of us.

I glanced out the window and gasped because there was one more blessing slowly coming down the drive toward the house.

A moving truck. And I was crossing my fingers that it was

actually our household goods inside the tractor-trailer this time.

* * *

WANT MORE? Sign up for my newsletter and never miss a new release!

The next book in the Reckless Camper Cozy Mystery Series, Death Is On The Menu, releases February 28th!

ABOUT THE AUTHOR

Libby Howard lives in a little house in the woods with her sons and two exuberant bloodhounds. She occasionally knits, occasionally bakes, and occasionally manages to do a load of laundry. Most of her writing is done in a bar where she can combine work with people-watching, a decent micro-brew, and a plate of Old Bay wings.

For more information:
libbyhowardbooks.com/

ALSO BY LIBBY HOWARD

Locust Point Mystery Series:

The Tell All

Junkyard Man

Antique Secrets

Hometown Hero

A Literary Scandal

Root of All Evil

A Grave Situation

Last Supper

A Midnight Clear

Fire and Ice

Best In Breed

Cold Waters

Five for a Dollar

Lonely Hearts - coming in 2022

Reckless Camper Mystery Series -

The Handyman Homicide

Death is on the Menu

The Green Rush

Elvis Finds a Bone

ACKNOWLEDGMENTS

Special thanks to Lyndsey Lewellen for cover design and Kimberly Cannon for editing.

In memory of my mother who was my biggest fan and my partner-in-crime.

Lightning Source UK Ltd.
Milton Keynes UK
UKHW010846070223
416609UK00003B/949